I0552279

Banshee
CHARMER

From the Files of the Otherworlder Enforcement Agency

TIFFANY ALLEE

This book is a work of fiction. Names, characters, places, and incidents are the product of the author's imagination or are used fictitiously. Any resemblance to actual events, locales, or persons, living or dead, is coincidental.

Copyright © 2012 by Tiffany Allee. All rights reserved, including the right to reproduce, distribute, or transmit in any form or by any means. For information regarding subsidiary rights, please contact the Publisher.

Entangled Publishing, LLC
2614 South Timberline Road
Suite 109
Fort Collins, CO 80525
Visit our website at www.entangledpublishing.com.

Covet is an imprint of Entangled Publishing, LLC.

Edited by Kerry Vail
Cover design by Curtis Svehlak
Cover art by Depositphotos

Manufactured in the United States of America

First Edition January 2012

Covet

To my mom, for always believing in me.

Chapter One

"What do we got, Aggie?"

The detective pulled a handkerchief from his back pocket and wiped at the sweat beaded on the top of his bald head. Some people might have assumed his reaction was nerves, but I knew it had to be hot in the house he'd just walked out of. Detective Joe Agrusa had been on the job for nearly twenty-five years, and only Mrs. Agrusa could make him nervous enough to sweat.

"What we got is a body. A weird one," he said.

"No shit? Here I was thinking you called me out because you're so damned fond of me."

He grinned, revealing a set of crooked but stain-free teeth. "You wish, freak hunter."

Aggie was human, shorter than me but at least twice my weight. I was usually the shortest woman in the room, which made the detective pretty damned short for a man. I looked down at him and snorted. "Fill me in."

He raised an eyebrow at my tone.

I kept my face straight, just barely. "Don't make me scream it out of you."

"Shit, Mac. All the years my wife's been nagging me and you think I'm not immune to a banshee? A half-assed one at that?"

The laugh bubbled out of my chest, and I choked it down. Only Aggie, of all the normals I worked with, would joke about my half-banshee status so easily. He realized what most cops didn't—that it didn't make me a whole helluva lot more dangerous than them. Oh, I could stun with a scream. Kill even, if given a lot of time or a weakened person. But I wasn't much more dangerous than a perp with a gun. Most of the normal cops just saw a freak. The thought smothered my lingering urge to laugh.

"Don't got any info for you, Mac. Not a crazed lycanthrope or goblin or anything like that. This one's downright creepy. You're gonna have to see for yourself."

I stifled a sigh. Aggie wasn't on the "freak squad," the affectionate term the normal cops gave the paranormal unit, but he'd been around long enough to know when to hand off a case to us. The fact that he was at a loss on this one didn't bode well. There wasn't much the old cop hadn't seen.

I glanced at a red Camry parked across the street. "Looks like Amanda beat me here."

"Yeah, she's inside already. Better get your ass movin'."

I muttered an expletive and trudged up to the front door. It stood ajar, held open with a cinderblock. A couple of uniforms stood in a corner chatting. One pointed down the hall when he saw me, but otherwise the rest ignored me. Some cops did their best to pretend the freak squad didn't exist, figuring the paranormal unit cops freaks by association.

Then again, most of us were freaks—and not by association.

A dark-haired Amazon stood over the bed, blocking the body from view. Amanda Franklin took three things very seriously: her job, her witchcraft, and her bodybuilding. All of which made her a great partner. We shared our hair color and penchant to exercise, but that's where our resemblance ended. My hair was wavy and generally pulled back out of my face, and Amanda towered over my five foot three inch frame.

The crime scene was in a standard master bedroom, nicely decorated if you didn't mind all surfaces covered in some sort of flora or fauna, both actual plants and plants printed on every available fabric in the room. Everything looked to be in its place and nothing indicated a struggle. Only a slight scent of something off touched the air. Not dead long, then.

I sidestepped to avoid a young guy carrying an evidence bag in one hand and a hard, metal specimen collection case in the other. A woman, mid-to-late twenties, lay spread-eagle on the bed, hands above her head, naked and wide-eyed. Her wrists were covered in purple and brown bruises, and her long, red hair fanned the pillow under her head. Other than the bruising, there were no obvious injuries.

"Vampire?" I asked. The bite marks from a vampire could be hidden, from a casual examiner anyway. The bite might be between her legs, behind a knee, on the back of her neck, or otherwise concealed under her body.

Amanda shook her head and tapped the file folder in her hand against her palm. "Medical Examiner just left." She pointed at the woman's legs. "Bruising on her thighs, mostly hidden by how she's lying, and on the wrists. No other marks visible. We'll know for sure when they get her back to the morgue, but I looked after the ME left and didn't see anything."

I frowned. If Amanda didn't find anything, there wasn't anything to find. "Are you thinking rape?"

"Well, it looks like she had sex before she died. Rape's a strong possibility considering the bruising. But the dead part—no clear explanation on that."

"Could be natural. Maybe a stroke or something. Her guy—if he was still here when it happened—took off because he was scared."

Amanda handed me the folder. "I'd agree with you, if this was the first one."

I flipped open the file. A woman's photo had been paper-clipped in front of the police report. She was brown-haired with glasses, and rather plain-looking by her picture, at least compared to the striking redhead on the bed.

"Why didn't we hear about this?"

"Normals called it death by natural causes. They didn't have any reason not to. Just like this, no marks, no blood. Less bruising on that one too, so they didn't see a reason to call us in. ME says both show signs of sex shortly before death."

"Hmm." I flipped through the first few pages of the file and skimmed. *Claire Simons, twenty-six years old, single, no kids. Found dead of apparent natural causes, nude with minor bruising on her legs.* No mention of bruising on her wrists.

"What do you think?" she asked.

"Not sure. The sex thing makes me think succubus, but I haven't heard of one killing her victims, and I've never heard of a succubus going for a woman—let alone two. Maybe an incubus, but incubi have been extinct since…"

"1850 or so."

"Sounds right. Vampire, we'd see some sort of marking." I sighed and looked back at the victim. Her lips were turned up slightly, like she was smiling. Creepy indeed. "You already call in for a sensitive?"

"Yeah, but we're looking at a couple of days." She grimaced. "Budget cuts."

"What about Holmes?"

Amanda shrugged. "Out of town."

It figured that the only sensitive on the squad would be unavailable. Sensitives could sense trace magic left behind when otherworlders used their powers. They were rare, and hiring one outside of the police department cost a pretty penny.

"Anything you can do?" I fanned myself with the file. No wonder Aggie had been sweating.

"Maybe, but forensics isn't going to let me muck up the scene with spell ingredients and a circle." Amanda pulled a small pair of scissors and a tiny plastic evidence baggy from her pocket. I turned to face the door and scanned the hall to make sure we were still alone, giving her a discreet thumbs-up behind my back.

A witch testing a victim's hair wasn't illegal or against regulations, even for an amateur witch, but with paperwork and procedures it could take upward of a week for approvals to be processed. Amateur witches like Amanda tested for licenses that allowed them to perform certain lower-tier spells. Unlike the rare Covenant witches, they weren't allowed to work for profit. Regulations didn't specifically prohibit Amanda from using magic to gain leads, but anything she did find would have to be duplicated by a contracted Covenant witch for it to be admissible in court.

After hearing a quick snip, I turned around. The evidence bag and scissors had disappeared back into Amanda's pocket. The victim was now short a few strands of hair, a small enough amount that no one was likely to notice.

A week was a long time to wait when hunting a potential serial killer.

"Maybe the women weren't murdered. Could just be an unfortunate coincidence," I said.

"Hah," Amanda replied without humor. "What's the first thing I told you when you made detective and were assigned as my partner?"

I opened the victim's file and looked at her picture. "There's no such thing as coincidences."

"Exactly."

"What're you thinking?"

"I agree it sounds like a succubus, but I want to see what the ME finds with the autopsy. Succubus wouldn't really fit if she had sex with a man right before she died."

"Unless the sex isn't connected with the death."

"Doubtful, but not impossible." Amanda stared at the woman as if the answers might materialize if she only looked hard enough.

"Divide and conquer?"

Amanda frowned. "Probably best. You talk to the Medical Examiner in the morning so I can work my mojo without Lieutenant Vasquez butting in."

The lieutenant didn't approve of Amanda using witchcraft for cases—then again, he didn't approve of much that wasn't strictly human in nature. And there were some definite stirrings in local governments as the Covenant pushed for making amateur witches use of magic in solving police cases illegal. Publicly, the Covenant questioned the expertise of amateur witches, but I suspected protecting their witches' pocketbooks was their real motivation. Their services cost police departments around the country significant cash.

"What, too sleepy to do it tonight?" A grin crept onto my face despite my best efforts to keep my expression blank.

Amanda raised an eyebrow at me. "I need my beauty sleep. You think shit this gorgeous comes without sacrifice?"

I barked out a quick laugh.

"Shops are closed. Unless you have some wormwood in your bra, we're SOL until morning," Amanda said.

"Sorry, left all my magical herbs in my other bra."

A smile flashed across Amanda's face, and she walked to the front of the house. I gave the victim one last glance and followed.

The two uniforms chatted in the corner. About their latest conquest or size of their guns, no doubt. Their conversation faded as we approached and the younger officer took in Amanda's fit body with barely concealed interest while the other kept his expression carefully neutral—a sure sign of a man trying not to sneer at the freaks. Amanda never failed to gain the attention of the younger generation. Those men weren't so bogged down by prejudice that a witch wasn't fair game. Their glances rarely shifted my direction. Having banshee powers—even stunted ones like mine—just wasn't sexy, despite my decent figure. Sure I didn't look any different from the average normal. But, my human appearance, as nicely packaged as it was, wasn't enough to counteract the fact that I was a half-banshee. And my banshee nature was well-known, especially among my fellow officers. Banshees had a reputation for being scary creatures—not sexy ones.

The crisp air licked my skin as we made our way to Amanda's car. Safely out of hearing range of our fellow officers, Amanda pulled a pack of cigarettes from her inner pocket and tapped one out. The fire from her lighter flashed and I blinked.

"Don't give me that look."

"I'm not looking at you," I grumbled, continuing to glare at her cigarette. Amanda only smoked when a case really got to her. Her one vice lingered despite her best efforts to control her life with a stranglehold grip. Considering the stress of the job, smoking was pretty damn harmless compared to what she could be doing to cope. It bugged me enough to give her a dirty look, but I wasn't about to criticize her aloud for a single weakness.

Not with everything she'd done for me.

I shook my head to clear my thoughts, and for the first time noticed her eyeliner and fading lipstick. "So how'd the date go?"

She crinkled her nose. "He canceled. I canceled the last one. I don't think a doctor and a cop are capable of dating. If my schedule isn't screwed, his is. Been over a month since we've met for a cup of coffee."

"Want a hug?" I opened my arms wide and grinned at her.

"Shit." She chuckled and tapped her cigarette lightly, releasing ash into the breeze.

I put my arms down and returned her smile. A van emblazoned with *Lake County Coroner* on the side pulled up and two youngish-looking men jumped out and headed for the back of the van. Damn, we were farther north than I'd realized. Those guys weren't going to be happy this body was headed to the city. One of the charms of working the paranormal unit was covering the entire Chicagoland area. Given our expertise, and most local cops' unwillingness to work OW cases, that area tended to cover Wisconsin to Iowa and far enough south of the city to see corn growing.

"You've come a long way, you know."

Unsure of how to respond, I stared at the ember tipping the end of her cigarette.

"You didn't even throw up."

"I haven't puked since my first case!" My face burned, hot against the coolness of the night air. "Besides, this vic *was* in one piece."

Amanda leaned against her car and smiled. "A heck of a first case. Nothing makes a mess quite like a lycanthrope catching her husband cheating."

Damn straight. They'd probably had to burn that house down.

• • •

The second I walked into my house, the hair stood on the back of my neck. Nothing seemed disturbed at first glance. My door was locked, and the small table next to the door still held the decorative box where I threw my keys every night. A print of Monet's *Garden Path* hung straight on the wall across from the front door. But something was wrong. A smell in the air maybe, or an imperfect silence that was usually perfect. Whatever the subtle clue, my subconscious translated it to a bad feeling in my gut. Not for the first time in my career as a cop, I wished I possessed the abilities of a sensitive.

I pulled my 9mm from its shoulder holster and crept into my living room. Light glowed from the dining room. Pretty certain I hadn't left a light on, I eased forward. I took a deep breath and held the air in my lungs, in case whatever waited for me couldn't be hurt with bullets.

I swung my gun up then rounded the corner into my dining room. A man—or something that looked like one anyway—sat at the oak table. He was reading a book. A cup of coffee rested on a coaster in front of him and he'd propped sock-covered feet on my table. Settled in, right at home.

I gaped, unsure of what to say. My face grew hot when I saw the cover of the book in his hand. A beautiful woman held in the arms of a tall, too-handsome hero with abs of steel graced the cover of the romance novel. I barely resisted the urge to shoot him. Who says I don't have fan-freaking-tastic self-control?

"Who are you?" I finally spluttered out.

He set the book down and smiled at me. It was one heck of a smile on one heck of a face. A strong jaw covered in five o'clock shadow, dark eyes, and a head of messy black hair set on a very fit, long body.

"Ah, Kiera McLoughlin, I presume?" I thought I detected a slight Irish lilt to his voice, but if he had an accent, it was subtle. He took his feet off the table, moving slowly.

"Presume away. Who are you and what are you doing in my house?"

His smiled turned into a full-on flirtatious grin. "Why don't you put your gun away so we can talk? About your interesting taste in books, perhaps."

I glared at him, face burning. Handsome or not, I was in charge in my own house. "No way, cupcake. Tell me who you are and I might consider putting my gun away."

He sighed, his chest pressing against his tight T-shirt. I glared harder.

"All right. My name is Aidan Byrne. I'm here to talk to you about the murders you're investigating."

I lowered my gun a few inches, more because of the weight than any level of trust I felt toward the stranger. "You a witness or something, Aidan? There're safer ways to report your info than breaking into a cop's house."

"Not a witness. I'm a cop, too. OWEA. I think we're looking for the same killer."

I raised my eyebrows. The Otherworlder Enforcement Agency was similar to the FBI in that they were selective in what they investigated. Generally, they took on paranormal-related crimes that crossed state lines or OW cases that needed resources outside of what a standard police department could pull together.

"So this perp has killed in other jurisdictions?"

"We think so."

"Show me some ID." I lowered my gun a few more inches and approached him carefully. "Please," I added, belatedly remembering that being polite to the jerk who broke into my house wouldn't kill me—but pissing off the OWEA might be the death of my career.

Raising one empty hand in the air, he leaned forward, reached into his back pocket with the other hand, and pulled out a leather badge and ID holder. He flipped it open and turned it so I could see.

I took the wallet from his hands and scanned its contents.

The dark badge glinted in the low light, and beneath it, nestled in a reflective piece of plastic, was an ID badge. The man's face grinned at me from behind the plastic, his dark hair and startling eyes clearly visible, even in the crappy ID photo. I shoved my gun into its holster and handed the wallet back to him. Fighting embarrassment, I grabbed the steamy romance novel he'd taken from the stack on the table, and shoved it onto the pile where it belonged.

"Okay, Agent Byrne, why did you think you needed to break into my house to talk to me about this case? OWEA running on hard times? Can't afford to supply agents with cell phones anymore?"

He put his badge away. "I wanted to talk to you tonight. We're strictly looking at this one on an unofficial basis." His easy smile disappeared and he shifted on the chair. "In fact, I'd appreciate it if you wouldn't mention the agency's involvement to anyone just yet."

I gave him my best cop stare. "Why come to me? Amanda's the senior investigator on this."

His grin returned. "She wasn't home yet."

Nothing like being the second-best choice. "You've got my attention. What are we looking for?"

"Wish I knew. What we do know is that it has been killing women all over the country for the last two years, at least."

I started. How many people had this sicko murdered? "Only women?" I pulled out my notepad and pen and sat down.

"Yes."

"How many?"

"Twelve that we know of."

I whistled under my breath. "Jesus. All...human?"

"No. Not all."

A chill ran down my spine and I looked up from my notepad. "It's killing otherworlders, too? What kinds?"

"A selkie and…"

"And?"

"A psychic. Not exactly an otherworlder, but close enough. One we'd consulted as a part of our investigation."

I set my pen down and leaned across the corner of the table separating us. "You think she was targeted because you talked to her?"

"Could be the killer thought she knew something. Maybe."

"Just the selkie and the psychic?" I picked my pen back up and struggled not to chew on it. A killer targeting other-worlders got under my skin. Not all of us were as powerful as vampires or Covenant witches, but most of us could take care of ourselves pretty well. A killer powerful enough to target OWs wasn't good.

"That we know of."

"Do you have the files?"

"I can't share those with you."

"Excuse me?"

"I'm sorry. Look. I would if I could, but I'll have to get an okay from my boss before I can do that."

His smooth, placating tone rubbed me the wrong way, but I didn't know him well enough to argue with him, even if he was lying. Besides, the OWEA had more bureaucracy in place than the city police.

"Well, get your permissions quickly. Jurisdictional bull isn't going to help us bring down this killer before it finds another victim." I thought about what Agent Byrne had said while a minute or two ticked by on the clock that hung from my dining room wall. Surprisingly he didn't interrupt.

"So a killer who targets humans and otherworlders who are as weak as humans. I'd like to see the fucker go after someone who can actually defend herself," I said, finally.

"Like a banshee?" His face hardened. "It's not a good idea to wish for things like that, Kiera."

I took a quick breath. So what if he knew about my half-banshee status? It might not be common knowledge, but it was hardly a secret. "Everyone calls me Mac."

"I prefer Kiera." He stared at me until I felt uncomfortable, and looked down. "We don't even know if they were targeted on purpose. The selkie, anyway. Neither was open about what they were."

"Not even the selkie?"

"She was trying to mainstream. A college student." He leaned forward and I resisted the urge to move in toward him. "Look. This guy is bad news. At the very least we have a serial killer. One who can kill without leaving a mark. You're not going to find any poison in your new victim, no other indicators beyond what you saw at the crime scene."

"This *guy*? Do you know something I don't?"

He shrugged. "Just going with the odds."

I raised an eyebrow. He was probably right. I considered telling him that Amanda was working her mojo on the victim's hair, but dismissed the idea. No way was I going to share every detail of my investigation with him while he kept his files to himself. "So no marks, no poison. Almost certainly some kind of freak."

He grimaced at the normally derogatory term for otherworlders and I realized that he was probably a freak himself. Most OWEA agents were. It gave them a better chance of survival, and normals tended to congregate toward the FBI or other less OW-centric organizations.

"It's the only thing that makes sense," he said.

"Were they all raped?"

"We couldn't confirm rape, but they all had sex shortly before they died."

"Confirmation enough for me."

· · ·

I parked in the only free space left adjoining the Medical Examiner's building. I pulled my jacket tighter, and walked to the front door. Aidan leaned against the gray building. Dark glasses adorned his face, despite the overcast skies. At my approach, he pushed off the wall and flashed me a grin.

I almost tripped.

I recovered my footing, and then frowned at him. "What are you doing here?"

"Helping you investigate, of course. Agencies working together." He waved his hand around. "All that jazz."

"Fine. But you'll let me do the talking."

He gave a mocking bow and gestured for me to go ahead of him into the building.

The stark decor in Dr. Martinson's office fit his profession. Gray floors and white walls combined with an old metal desk and black chairs to create an ambiance appropriate for visiting the Medical Examiner. It suited my mood after the embarrassing evening I'd had. There had been no way to recover after Aidan found my romance novel collection. His slight grin reminded me until he left, as if mocking my tough-cop disguise. But it wasn't a persona, dammit. I'd show him I was more than capable.

"Doc, surprised to find you in your office," I said.

In his mid-fifties, handsome and silver-haired, he looked every bit the distinguished doctor he was and not at all like what most would expect from a man whose job required him to examine the dead.

He gestured to the chairs in front of his desk and we sat. I pushed down the temptation to glance at Aidan. Something about the man drew my gaze and made me very aware of how much time had passed since my last date.

Dr. Martinson looked up from the folder he'd been reading and said, "I'm afraid my job is more paperwork than actual work these days. Who's your friend?"

"He's with me. Tagging along." Not exactly a lie.

The doctor gave Aidan a quick nod and turned his attention back to me. "What can I do for you, Detective?"

"Woman brought in last night, Rebecca Anderson. No obvious marks on the body other than bruising."

"Coffee?" He gestured toward his door. I'd seen the coffee pot on our way in. It sat on a table in the hallway between the Medical Examiner's office and the morgue.

I shook my head. Morgue coffee? No thanks.

He grabbed a file from the top of his desk and flipped it open. "Anderson. Twenty-three years old. No immediate indicators of cause of death. Initial exam shows sexual activity shortly before she died, bruising on her thighs and wrists."

"When's the autopsy?"

"Probably get to her tonight or first thing tomorrow morning."

I wanted to grumble, but managed to control myself. Pissing off the Medical Examiner, especially in front of an audience, wasn't a good idea considering how often I had to deal with him. He could make my job a lot harder than it needed to be. I glanced at Aidan, half expecting him to comment. His eyes were on me, intense and focused. My breath caught in my throat. I swallowed and looked down at my hands.

"Had another death, couple of weeks back. Lot of similarities. Got anything on that one?" I asked, relieved to have a distraction from the intensity of Aidan's gaze.

"Name?"

"Claire Simons."

Dr. Martinson pushed his rolling office chair back from his desk and slid over to a filing cabinet. "A couple of weeks, you said?"

I flipped out my notepad. "Yeah, on the twelfth."

"Should still have her paperwork then." He flipped through the cabinet and then pulled out a file.

I frowned at the size. I risked a quick glance at Aidan, but his attention was focused on the doctor.

Dr. Martinson slid back to his desk and opened her folder. He slipped on a pair of reading glasses, and never lifted his eyes from the file. "Got the blood work on her. An autopsy was conducted."

"Who was the main on the case?"

"Joe Agrusa."

I snorted. No wonder he'd called us in on the new case. He'd seen it before. "Okay, any highlights?"

"Twenty-six. Some bruising. Sexual intercourse not long before her death, but no fluids present—he used a condom. No indication of force. Tox reports showed only a small amount of alcohol in her system, no other drugs."

"Cause of death?"

"Unknown."

"That's it? Unknown?"

"That's it. We didn't find anything that indicated cause of death."

I sighed. "Great. How about oh-dubs? Any odd energies on the body?"

"OW procedures weren't run," he said, carefully pronouncing each letter of the acronym for otherworlder measures as if the words left a bad taste on his tongue. "There were no indicators of an otherworlder being involved. Her parents said she was fully human and had no involvement with any…OWs."

Freaks. *Why not say what you mean, doctor?* "Okay so there's no clear COD, but why wouldn't you run OW procedures?" I copied the doctor's precise pronunciation, unable to keep the irritation I felt out of my tone. I shot Aidan a glance, but he remained silent, his face as close to expressionless as I'd seen it. A lot of help he was.

"We don't run them if we don't have a reason to. Psychics, sensitives, witches…they're expensive. Nothing about this body indicated a reason."

"Except for the fact she was dead! And not even thirty years old! Jesus, Doc." I drew up my arm, but managed to stop myself from slamming my fist down on his desk.

Dr. Martinson whipped the file closed. "I don't make the rules, Detective. I just follow them."

"I'm going to need a copy of that report."

Dr. Martinson nodded curtly. He frowned at me and left the office, presumably to find someone to make a copy. So much for not pissing him off.

As soon as the door clicked shut behind the doctor I turned to Aidan. "What the hell? When did you turn into the strong, silent type?"

"Didn't you tell me to let you do the talking?" White teeth flashed as his grin returned. "You seemed to be doing fine on your own. Besides, we learned what we needed."

"Oh yeah, what's that?"

"That your killer has the same M.O. as mine." He leaned forward in his chair and swiped a tuft of lint from my jacket.

I drew in a quick breath and searched my mind for something clever to say. Failing that, I pulled my cell phone from my jacket pocket. Then I tapped my foot. Finally, after the forth ring, Amanda's voice mail picked up.

"Hey it's me." I glanced at Aidan. "Did you find that thing you needed?" I considered mentioning the OWEA, but decided against it. Some things were better discussed in person, and preferably not in front of Aidan. "Meet me for lunch? Normal spot, noon. Call me if you can't make it."

• • •

The doctor returned with the file, a sour expression on his face as he passed it to me. Without looking at the paper-work, I got up from the chair and then nodded at the doctor. Aidan and I stepped out of his dreary office. Halfway down the hall, a woman faced away from us toward the morgue. Great, just what I needed. Given Amanda's opinion that a succubus could be involved, this woman was almost definite-ly there for me.

I looked back at Aidan. His eyes were locked on the woman as well. I started to tell him to close his damned mouth, and then decided against it. Guys couldn't help staring at this particular woman.

"I'll see you later. Errands to run," Aidan said, surprising me. I'd half expected him to ask about the woman his eyes were still glued to.

"Whatever," I murmured to his back. Pivoting, I headed for the morgue.

I would have recognized the frame of the succubus leaning against the wall anywhere. Marisol Whitfield was nearly as tall as Amanda, maybe five feet nine, and closer to six feet in her conservatively heeled shoes. Despite their similar heights, her well-endowed chest and curvy frame distinguished her from the rest of the police officers on the freak squad, especially Amanda. Where Amanda was hard, Marisol was soft.

I frowned at her, and she gave me a smug grin.

"Here to see the doc?" I asked.

"Nope. Here to see you." She flipped a long blond lock behind her shoulder with practiced ease and fluttered her sparkling blue eyes at me. She couldn't help the succubus sex appeal that always draped her, but it irritated me anyway. "Well, here to see a body with you, to be more precise."

"Want to get some coffee to go?" I waved at the pot sitting near us in the hallway that led to the morgue.

Marisol blanched, and the horrified look that briefly crossed her face made me realize I wasn't the only one who considered morgue coffee to be the most disgusting idea ever. Her expression almost made an errand that was probably a waste of my time worthwhile.

"Vasquez sent you?"

She gave me a short nod and her superior grin faded.

"I'm to accompany you to the morgue to look at the body. Guess he thinks I can offer a unique point of view."

I grimaced, covering my expression with a wave of the folder the doctor had given me with the copies I'd requested. Leave it to Lieutenant Vasquez to send someone to consult just because she happened to be a member of a species who could pull off the murder. Somehow, even after years of working in the paranormal unit, Vasquez couldn't get the idea out of his head that all of us freaks knew each other. He also seemed convinced we had some sort of extra preternatural sense that allowed us to solve a murder without normal necessities, like evidence.

We reached the morgue and I wondered if Amanda had filled in the lieutenant. It almost certainly hadn't been Aggie. He talked to the paranormal cops more than the average normal detective, but that didn't mean he went out of his way to do it. Did Lieutenant Vasquez know everything? Probably, except for the spell Amanda intended to cast using the victim's hair. Amanda was pretty conscious of keeping every *i* dotted and *t* crossed, and that included keeping her boss in the loop.

Claire Simons's body had been released to her family, but Rebecca Anderson still rested in the morgue. A somber-faced young man wearing light blue scrubs met us at the entryway. "She's ready for you. Set up straight through there."

I glanced at Marisol, a look she pointedly ignored, and followed her into the room. Rebecca appeared a little worse than she had the night before, even with most of her body covered by a sheet. Her pale skin seemed grayer, and the fluorescent lights dimmed her bright red hair.

"Guess this is where you use your succubus super sense

to figure out if it was one of your kind who did this, huh?"

The laugh that bubbled out of her chest seemed to surprise her more than it did me, and she went silent after only a few seconds. Her plump, brightly colored lips turned up. A bit less smugness remained than she usually wore when she glanced at me before turning her attention back to Rebecca.

"Vasquez wants me to look, so that's what I'm going to do." She shrugged and placed her hands on the table, and then bent down to examine Rebecca's face. She tugged the fabric away and moved her eyes across the body, gaze slowing over the bruises on Rebecca's wrists.

I felt a momentary pang for Marisol. Vasquez's lack of knowledge about otherworlders astounded me, considering the fact that he ran the unit responsible for investigating OW-related crimes in the entire Chicago area. Succubi weren't sensitives and Marisol couldn't sense anything different than a normal cop examining the victim would, even if a succubus had killed the woman. Succubi, to my knowledge, had two powers. They exuded a sexual vibe—some more subtly than others—and they could pull power from a person they were having sex with. Enough to kill someone, perhaps. Someone like our victims. But they were as sensitive to psychic energy as I was—meaning not at all.

Her lack of concern over touching the body with her manicured nails surprised me. I crossed my arms and examined the succubus as she examined the victim. I shouldn't have expected her to be queasy around the dead—she was a cop, after all. The succubus was a detective who had been at the rank longer than I had, though she couldn't be more than a year or two my senior.

Marisol threw the sheet back over the body with a speed

that made me start. When she turned to face me, all the friendliness had disappeared from her expression. A small amount of perspiration touched her brow.

"All right," she said. "I've seen enough."

"And?"

"And what? You don't honestly think I can just look at her and know how she died, do you?"

"No, but—"

She waved her hand at me, cutting off my argument. Then she turned on her heel and left the room, slamming the door behind her.

I followed her, leaving the flustered technician in our wake. I finally caught up in the hallway outside of the morgue. "Hey," I called, and she slowed before stopping and turning to face me.

"Sorry I was rude," she said. "I don't like dead bodies. I wanted to get out of there." Her expression appeared open again. She didn't smile exactly, but her eyes were wide and filled with emotion, as if the hardness I'd glimpsed before had never crossed her face.

I frowned at her, unconvinced. The body hadn't seemed to bother her when we'd first gone into the room. Maybe she'd just hid it? Not all cops handled dead bodies and blood and gore as well as others. It was possible she couldn't deal with that kind of thing, or at least preferred to deal with it as little as she could manage in her job.

"Sure, no problem." The added paleness of her skin and sweating certainly supported her assertion, but it was the fact that her reaction fit my impression of her that convinced me. First impressions weren't always right, but I was good at reading people. For now, I'd have to trust my gut.

I glanced at my watch. "Look, I have to get to a lunch appointment. I know you can't say for sure, but do you think the killer could be a succubus?"

"Succubi don't kill their prey; it's unheard of." She flattened some invisible wrinkles on her jacket with her palms. "I'll let the lieutenant know." She turned and headed for the door.

I reached the parking lot before I realized she hadn't actually answered my question.

As I unlocked my car, my cell phone rang. I frowned at the unfamiliar number, and then flipped it open.

"McLoughlin."

"Hello, Kiera." The smooth voice on the other end of the line was unmistakable.

"Did you forget something, Agent Byrne?" I tried, and failed, to keep the snippiness out of my tone.

"Just checking in. Did you get a look at the body?"

"No, I thought I'd take a quick trip to Hawaii instead. I have an appointment to get to. I'll call you later."

He chuckled and I snapped the phone shut. The man thought he was so damn charming.

Chapter Two

The Grill House was packed for lunch. They were always busy, but they were quick, good, and cheap. They were also close to the precinct so a lot of cops ate there. Lisa, our normal waitress, waved me in and I helped myself to a booth.

"Meeting someone?" she asked, pulling a pen out from behind her ear. She managed to pull off short, spiky blue hair without looking like a punk.

"Amanda."

"Cool. Haven't seen her yet. Wanna order or wait?"

I went through my mental to-do list. "Cheeseburger and fries. Coke. Hold the onions on the burger, extra pickles."

She made a quick note on her order pad. "Got it," she said, and then disappeared into the crowd.

I chewed on the end of my pen and glanced through my notepad while I waited for Amanda and my food. No obvious cause of death, no markings. No poison or other oddities in the blood work. How else could you kill a person? Drain them of their life force. And how did the perp get the victims back to their homes? I'd have a lot more to go on if Aidan would hurry up with the other victims' files. Damn home invader. Why on earth would he snoop through my books? Could the man be as handsome as I remembered? No, I was under the influence of little sleep on top of no dates in… sheesh, nearly a year.

"Mind if I join you?" The masculine voice pulled me from my thoughts. It took me a moment to focus on the man in front of me. Taking my silence as assent, Aidan sat down across from me in the booth.

My cheeks heated. They were probably already red. *Stop it*, I told myself. *There's no way he could know what you were thinking.* "I'm expecting someone."

"Your partner?"

"What're you doing, following me?" I glared at him, irritated that he was more attractive every time I saw him.

"I didn't need to follow you. You're terribly predictable. The second you said 'normal spot' to Amanda's voice mail I had your restaurant pegged." He gave me a sexy grin.

I opened my mouth but no words came out.

"You look like a fish when you do that."

I snapped my jaw shut. "Why are you here?" My voice came out sounding shrill.

"Came to see what you dug up. Where's your partner?" He looked around me as if searching for her in the back of the restaurant.

I pushed down a twinge of jealousy. Why wouldn't he be interested in Amanda? Most guys were. And not many noticed a girl with banshee blood, except to make sure they gave her a wide berth. I shook my head to clear my thoughts.

What was I doing? He was just a jerky cop. A good-looking jerky cop, but still. I made a mental note to get myself a date as soon as we solved this case. Obviously, my lack of a sex life was finally getting to me. I turned my attention back to Aidan.

He had on a bemused expression, like he knew what I was thinking.

I scowled. "Amanda isn't here yet."

"Well? Did you find out anything from looking at the body?"

"Probably nothing that will surprise you."

"Try me."

"Nothing other than what the coroner said. No obvious cause of death on the first victim or the second. They both had sex before they died. No DNA left from her attacker. No identifiable poisons in her system. No drugs, only a small amount of alcohol. Looking at the body didn't tell me anything new." As Lisa approached with my Coke, I straightened my posture, embarrassed that I hadn't noticed I'd leaned toward Aidan as I spoke.

"Hi there," she said, giving Aidan a smile. "What can I get for you?" She bent over, putting her hand on the table, her back to me. More specifically with the way she rested, her backside.

I frowned. She made the simple question sound like an invitation. What was it with this guy anyway? I cocked my head to the side and raised an eyebrow at Aidan.

"Iced tea, please. No lemon."

"Sure thing." I couldn't see the expression she wore when she sashayed away, but it was probably pretty damn welcoming.

"Anyway," I said, more loudly than I needed to. Aidan

was staring, not at the waitress, but at me. The annoying grin stuck to his face. "As I was saying. We haven't found anything that you probably didn't already know."

"What about oh-dubs?" He flashed a quick smile at Lisa as she dropped off his drink but didn't move his eyes from my face. Looking miffed, Lisa sauntered away. Probably to spit on my cheeseburger.

"They didn't run any OW measures on the first vic. They'll run them on the second, or I'll be kicking someone's ass."

He grunted and took a long drink of his tea.

Lisa showed up with my cheeseburger and fries. She gave Aidan a long look as she walked away, nearly running over another waitress. I checked my watch. Twelve thirty.

"Guess your partner isn't coming." He stared at me with his dark blue eyes and a shiver ran down my spine.

Get a grip, Mac. I looked at my burger, removing the top bun. It appeared saliva-free.

"I'm looking forward to meeting her."

"I'll bet you are," I muttered and then took a big bite of my burger.

He coughed and covered his mouth with a fist. It sounded suspiciously like a muffled laugh. He set a white business card next to my plate. It was blank, save for his name and a phone number. "So you can contact me." He sipped his iced tea.

The number was from out of state, but I didn't recognize the area code. This seemed like as good a time as any to ask what kind of otherworlder he was. The question was rude, but I needed to know who—what—I was dealing with. Warming him up with small talk seemed best, so I took a stab at it. "This your first time in Chicago?" I took another bite of my juicy burger, catching a bit of the grease with my tongue as it tried to dribble down my chin.

"Nope," he said.

My cell phone began vibrating, and I glared at Aidan while I reached for it. The caller ID listed Amanda's number. About time. I flipped the phone open a second too late, so I hit the send button to call her back. I muttered another expletive when her automated message blared in my ear, and then pressed the end button without leaving a message.

"Your partner?"

"Yep," I said.

My cell beeped and an icon flashed on the screen. Great, she was leaving me a message as I was calling her. I hit the button to listen to my voice mail and put the phone to my ear.

"Hey Mac, it's me." Amanda sounded tired. No doubt from a night of witchery. "Won't be able to meet you today. Following up on that sample. Can you go interview the vic's boyfriend?" She rattled off the guy's information. "I'll be in touch."

I snapped the phone shut and cursed under my breath. Could she have been any more vague?

"Going to see a man about a girl." I took a long drink from my straw. "Latest vic's boyfriend. Want to come?"

• • •

The apartment complex wasn't in the nicest part of town, but it didn't scream projects either. The door didn't require buzzing, so we walked in without a hitch. An old man sat on a bench reading a newspaper in what passed for a lobby. The dingy room seemed like an odd place to hang out and read, particularly with the moldy scent in the air, but to each his own.

The elevator had an OUT OF ORDER sign taped to it, handwritten in red marker on a sheet of white paper that looked like it had typing on the back. Someone took their recycling seriously. Suppressing a sigh and telling myself exercise did the body good, I waved at Aidan to follow me and trudged up the stairs to the fourth floor.

I rapped on the door to apartment 404. I heard a shuffling from inside, and the *shink* of a security chain. The door popped open, revealing a man in his early twenties. Tall, blond, and lean. Definitely a pretty boy, even wearing only a T-shirt and basketball shorts, his prettiness was obvious. He and the redhead must have turned more than a few heads together.

"Jason Hill?"

"Yeah?" His bleary eyes peered out at me, as if hoping to see someone else. A faint smell of alcohol flowed from his breath. His hair looked like it hadn't been combed yet today and he definitely needed a shave.

"I'm Detective Kiera McLoughlin. You spoke to my partner on the phone?"

"Oh yeah, sorry." He backed away from the door and motioned for us to enter. "It's just. You know, not every day you find out…" He took a deep breath.

"I'm sorry for your loss," I said, walking through the doorway that led directly into the living room. A small kitchen sat off to the side, and in such an enclosed space it reminded me of a cave. There was no dining table—or enough space for one really—and a loveseat and coffee table seemed to round out his furnishings. I couldn't see into the bedroom, but I would bet his mattress sat directly on the floor.

"Sorry for the mess." He tossed some clothes off the couch to make room for us to sit.

"No problem. We just have a few questions for you. Shouldn't take too much of your time." *Not that you look like you're going somewhere anytime soon.*

"I want to help."

I sat down on one side of the short couch, and he sat on the other end. Aidan remained in the entryway between the hall and living room. He leaned against the wall and watched us, his expression neutral.

As I pulled out my notebook and flipped it to a blank page, I studied Jason Hill. He didn't look like an other-worlder, but you couldn't always tell by a person's appearance. He didn't feel like one either. My gut told me he was a plain human. I wished again for the powers of a sensitive.

"When was the last time you saw Rebecca?"

"Few days ago. I stayed at her place…most nights."

"Why didn't you stay last night?" *Or see her the few nights before?*

"I was supposed to, but she called me last week and said she was doing something for work out of town. Then she called me yesterday afternoon. Said something had come up. She was…" He stared down at his hands.

"What?"

"She was different. She said…she'd found somebody else." He finished in a rush. "But that wasn't like her. Some-one made her say it. I know—"

"It's okay." I patted him awkwardly on the shoulder. I hated this part. "Take your time."

Jason pulled in a ragged breath. "We've been together nearly two years. She wouldn't drop me over the phone. She sounded…off."

"Off?"

"Rebecca was a calm person. People who didn't know her well thought she was cold. She wasn't! She just wasn't one to share how she felt with the whole world." He looked up at me and tears welled in his eyes. "She was elated, al-most…crazy in her excitement over this new guy."

I frowned. Either she was a real bitch to dump her boy-friend over the phone or she'd been under some sort of in-fluence. Unless Jason here did something to really piss her off, I would be willing to bet on the former.

"This might sound like an odd question, but did she spe-cifically say she'd met a new guy?" Aidan asked.

Jason jerked out of his reverie. "I—" He stared into space for a few moments. "I guess not. She said she had someone new in her life. I didn't think to ask…I mean she wasn't into chicks, you know?"

Jason started sobbing into his hands. I patted him on the shoulder again and told him to cry it out.

I glanced over my shoulder as the man shook against me. Sorrow laced Aidan's features. His eyes met mine and he stiffened. Then his face relaxed into its normal expression. A slight grin, and eyes that revealed nothing.

· · ·

By the time we left Jason Hill's house, the material of my blouse clung to my shoulder, soaked with the man's tears. It would dry stiff and odd-looking. And now most of the af-ternoon was gone. Mentally drained, all I wanted to do was go home and knock back enough beers to make this day disappear for a while.

Aidan said something about double-checking one of the crime scenes and then disappeared into his rented Jeep. I tried Amanda's cell again and left her a less-than-civil message. I wasn't her keeper or her boss; she didn't have to report in to me, but it was still irritating.

I downed a beer when I got home, and then nursed the second one. This case was a mystery, and unlike most people I didn't like a good mystery until I had it solved. I flipped open my laptop, waiting a moment for the screen to brighten. My cell phone rang, and I answered it without looking at the number.

"McLoughlin."

"Mac, Astrid here." Her voice was gruffer than normal, like she was angry about something. I couldn't recall the last time I'd heard her angry. Hell, I was pretty sure I'd never seen the woman's temper well enough to know for sure she had one.

"Shit, you back in town already?" I couldn't keep the happiness out of my voice. Our department had access to exactly one sensitive, and I couldn't pretend I wasn't thrilled to hear from her.

"Look Mac, I can't really chat right now." Oh yeah, definite irritation dripped from the normally placid woman's tone. "I got a look at one of your vics, Rebecca Anderson."

"And?" I asked, losing all interest in what could have irritated our mousy little sensitive enough to make her angry.

"And she's been drained of nearly all of her psychic energy. Her life force. Tentatively, I'd say that's your COD."

I pinched the bridge of my nose. "Doesn't the body naturally lose energy after death?"

"Yes, but that process takes weeks, not days. I couldn't get a feel for what kind of OW might have done it. There wasn't enough psychic energy left in her for any magic to cling to." A loud crash sounded and yelling followed it. "Look Mac, I gotta go. That's all I know. Good luck."

The line went dead before I could spit out any more questions. I gave the phone a final glare and then turned my attention to the laptop.

I typed in my password and then clicked the icon for the Otherworlder Information Database. The OWID held data on general otherworlder statistics, not information on specific criminals. Facts like when certain species were seen last and where, their abilities and danger levels, and how to subdue them.

I searched for "psychic draining" and watched the ticker bar fill on my screen. I downed the rest of beer number two, and seriously considered standing up to get another before the page drove me mad with its slowly loading bar.

The list made me frown. Wraiths didn't explain the sex issue, unless one somehow became corporeal. That didn't make sense. Wraiths were mindless and had no self-control. We'd be seeing a lot more victims. Baku fed psychically but focused on dreams. They could drive a person insane but they wouldn't kill them outright. And again, the sex angle made no sense.

Incubi were on the list as well. Although they had been extinct for over a hundred and sixty years, everything else fit. Except for the fact that they weren't known for draining people to the point of death. Succubi were listed too. The female version of the incubus could only produce female offspring. Like incubi, succubi were averse to killing their food.

I scrolled down the list, and saw too many species to go through. Nothing other than the wraiths, baku, incubi, and succubi were known for being powerful enough to actually kill something through draining. I clicked in the "search within results" box and typed "sex." The enter key made a loud click in my otherwise silent house. Rather than pull my hair out watching the page load, I went and grabbed another beer. When I got back to the laptop, there were only two species left on the list.

I rubbed my eyes, not surprised, but I'd hoped for some beastie out there I hadn't heard of that fit the bill. Nothing else even came close. Not a creature anyone knew about, anyway. Every otherworlder species that existed, now or in the past, claimed its share of space in the OWID. As the words "incubus" and "succubus" flashed at me from the screen, I wondered how I was going to convince anyone that a succubus was running around killing women while making it look like her victims had been killed by a man, or that incubi weren't extinct after all.

A loud knock startled me. I snapped the laptop shut and made my way to the door. The vision through the peephole made me sigh.

"Well hello, beautiful," Aidan said when I pulled the door open. He held up a six-pack of beer and waved the bottles hypnotically at me. "Can I come in?"

I waved him inside, grabbing a bottle as he passed, and then followed him to the dining room.

"Did you find anything we missed?" I asked, already knowing the answer. The paranormal unit ran a tight ship.

"No, your team was very thorough. What did you find out?" He picked up the bottle opener I'd left on the table, and held his palm out. I gave him my beer and he flipped the lid off, then handed it back to me before opening his own.

"Our local sensitive checked out the most recent vic. She was drained of her life force. Astrid's calling that COD." I gestured at the laptop. "I'm seeing a few things that can kill that way, but only a couple fit."

"Let me guess: succubi and their incubi cousins."

I took a sip of my beer. "Yup."

He hesitated. "Look, I know this is a little rude to ask, but…your banshee powers, do they extend to the visions?"

I narrowed my eyes. "No. Why is that relevant?"

"It might come in handy if they did."

"Do you really think that if I got visions of people dying before it happened that I'd be in this line of work? Hell, if I was a true banshee, do you think I'd be living with humans?"

He shrugged, obviously uncomfortable. "I knew it was a long shot, but I had to ask."

"Do you know how banshee society operates?"

"Probably not as well as you. I know that they can usually see when someone near them is going to die. And their screams are fatal."

"That's true—to a certain extent. Their screams can kill and, unfortunately, most banshees scream when they're hit with a vision. That's why they live away from humans."

"But all banshees are women, right?" He grinned. "How do they, you know, make little banshees?"

"Some journey out to mate with humans. They only produce female children, and only keep the ones who inherit their full range of abilities. The rest are discarded as half-breeds."

"Discarded?"

"Oh yes," I said bitterly. "Literally. Like trash."

"I'm surprised law enforcement around their reservations allows them to journey into human territories, let alone toss out their young."

"It's not legal, but they're difficult to police. I mean, I wouldn't want to try to stop a full-blooded banshee. Plus, they look like humans. So unless you catch one crossing the reservation line, they can be hard to ID." I rested the cold beer against my cheek. What was this? My third? No wonder I was so chatty.

"So what happened with you?" Aidan murmured.

I shrugged. "My dad was in Ireland for the summer. He'd just graduated high school and wanted to see his homeland or some such nonsense before college. He met my mom in a small village. He stayed, and so did she. He doesn't talk about it much, but I guess they cared for each other. She cared enough to leave me with him after I was born instead of tossing me into the ocean."

"Well, you seem to have turned out okay without her in your life." He leaned toward me, forearms resting against the table in front of him. "Gotta be kind of lonely, though. I don't think I've ever met a half-banshee before. I've met a couple full-blooded ones. Well, fully powered ones, really. But never what they call half-bloods. I've never met anyone quite like you."

Well, wasn't I special? I cleared my throat. "Yeah, well, I was raised by a good man." I had to get the subject off my parentage before I got weepy. Damn, definitely too many beers. "Did you get along with your family?"

Pain flared behind his eyes, gone as quickly as it had appeared. "I never knew my dad. He…wasn't exactly the marrying kind."

I opened my mouth to press him for more information, but stopped. An angry Aidan I could push, but I wasn't sure I was ready to deal with a troubled one.

"Look," I said, finally. "Let's get back to the case. The only OWs I can figure for it are succubi and incubi. Have you come across anything else in your investigation that might fit?"

"Nope."

• • •

The headache pressing against the back of my eyes hadn't improved much with my first cup of coffee, and neither had my mood. I leaned against the wall in front of the office door, holding my second cup in one hand and an open book on succubi in the other, with a file tucked tenuously between my arm and chest. I didn't have high hopes that a headache would be the worst of my problems today.

The door clicked open and a man who appeared to be in his late twenties stepped out wearing a dark suit, sans tie. The tailored outfit looked too pricey for a cop, and I could have ID'd him from that alone. "Mac," Detective Claude Desmarais said as he walked past.

"Claude," I muttered to the detective, and headed into the office he'd just vacated.

"Sit down, Mac." Lieutenant Vasquez, the Hispanic man behind the desk, was only an inch or two taller than me, but made up for his lack of height with broad shoulders and large biceps, although his rounding midsection revealed that his job now required him to work from a desk every day. A full head of dark hair belied his age—I knew for a fact he was in his mid-fifties. I often wondered if he dyed his hair, but that wasn't something I was willing to ask him even if I'd had a few beers.

"Lieutenant," I said, sitting on the chair across from him. I set my coffee and book on the desk, gripping the file in my hands.

After signing the paper he'd been reading, he looked up at me. "Okay, what do you got?"

"I think we've got an incubus. Possibly a succubus." No one would ever call me indirect.

He leaned back in his chair and studied me. I stared right back at him, tempering my usual glare to a solid cop face.

He let out a muttered string of expletives, his voice low enough that I couldn't make out any word but "freaks." Then he leaned back in his chair and rubbed his face. "Aren't incubi supposed to be extinct?"

"They're supposed to be, yes."

The muscles in his jaw tensed and he crossed his arms. "Okay, tell me."

"We've got two victims here, and several more who could be connected in other jurisdictions. I'm looking into it. All the vics are women. All dead with no physical cause. All had sex before they died. I've got oh-dubs going on the latest vic this week. Oh, and Astrid called last night and confirmed the woman had been drained of her life force and that's likely what killed her."

"You think the killer isn't a succubus because?"

"Did Whitman tell you it was?"

"She denied it, but Amanda said it was a possibility when she called me from the scene."

I frowned. Could Marisol really say a succubus hadn't

killed her? "Spermicide from a condom was found in our first vic. Once they get around to the autopsy I'm sure they'll find it in the second, too."

"That doesn't necessarily mean it isn't a succubus, or some other kind of copycat freak who's worked out a way to mimic an incubus's M.O. Would be a good way to throw us off the trail."

"Could be. I haven't ruled anything out—especially not the possibility that it's a succubus. The only other OWers I've found that could psychically drain someone to the point of death are wraiths and baku. But neither fit the sex angle. If we had a wraith on our hands we'd see several victims every night, all clumped together. Baku feed off dreams, slowly driving their victims insane. There wasn't anything slow about this. A succubus or incubus is the only thing that fits." I paused, trying to figure out the right wording that wouldn't make Vasquez laugh his ass off at a cop being so convinced by her feelings. "My gut says incubus," I said, finally.

Vasquez didn't agree or disagree with my gut, or with my analysis of the freaks capable of the murders. Instead he said, "So what're we looking at if it is an incubus?"

"Database seems to indicate they have pretty much the same powers as a succubus. They exude sex appeal, probably varies how much from incubus to incubus, just like with succubi. They can drain energy from their victims, which probably gives them additional power." I shrugged. "But one hopped up on the energy of so many victims? Hell, who knows what kind of power that could give him? There are stories of powerful incubi being able to control their victims with their power, but it's hard to separate fact from fiction when the latest info is over one hundred years old."

He held out his hand and I passed him the paperwork on the first victim, Claire Simons. While he perused the file, I nursed my second cup of coffee. The caffeine was finally kicking in against my headache. It wasn't winning yet but I had hope.

"All right," he said a few minutes later. Flipping the file closed, he passed it back to me over the table. "Let me know what else you find out. We need to nab this guy. And don't screw this up, Mac. If the killer really is an incubus then this case will make the news every-damn-where. We don't want to be the department that botches the takedown. We'll have to look into a contracted witch in a few days if you and Amanda don't make any headway. And while you're at it, tell her to call me. I haven't heard from her since her initial report after you guys left Rebecca Anderson's."

Dread swirled in my stomach, making me suddenly nauseous. It wasn't like Amanda to go this long without talking to me. Then again, it wasn't entirely *unlike* her either. But if Vasquez wanted me to pull her in, she hadn't been reporting to him either. Chances were she was fine, just doing a little undercover witchcraft that wasn't fully sanctioned, and rightfully laying low. I told that to my stomach, but it ignored me.

"Will do."

"You've got a suspect to question," he said. I got up from my chair. I raised an eyebrow and he added, "Desmarais will fill you in."

"Claude? Why's he involved?"

"It's a vamp lead."

"What the hell? There's no indication that these are vamp kills." I leaned toward him and lowered my voice.

"Seriously, Vasquez. I don't have time to follow a wild goose chase just because you don't like vamps."

Vasquez pushed away from his desk and leaned toward me. Redness crawled up his neck and his face tightened. "Don't push me, Mac. You'll follow up on this lead, or you'll find your ass behind a desk before you can say bloodsucker."

Chapter Three

Claude Desmarais stood in front of Interview Room Two with a folder tucked under one arm and a Styrofoam coffee cup in the opposite hand. At just over six feet tall, with light brown hair long enough to tuck behind his ears, the man looked more like a surfer or snowboarder than a dead man. Even with Claude's slightly pale skin, most would never guess he was a vampire. He didn't exude the aura of fear that rolled off most vamps.

He handed me the coffee when I approached and I nodded in thanks, placing the Styrofoam cup into the now-empty one I held in my hand. Vampires were the only type of undead who were classified as people, which meant they couldn't be discriminated against at work — though I'd never seen one working as a doctor or elementary school teacher. But laws were laws, so Vasquez had no choice but to keep Claude on the squad. Despite old lore to the contrary, banshees weren't undead, just people with an extra powerful set of lungs. I'd worked with Claude before and he was pretty decent, for a man who ate blood to stay alive.

"I'm perfectly capable of questioning a vampire on my own. Why is Vasquez insisting on your involvement?" I asked, shooting Claude a small smile to take the edge off my tone. I was still pissed at Vasquez, but that didn't mean I had to take it out on Claude. I concentrated on calming down and repeated my mantra in my head. *You're a fucking professional. You're a professional.*

"Because the suspect Vasquez has invited to join us is a Chevalier."

"There's a member of the Chevalier family in our interview room?" I gestured to the door next to him, trying to keep my voice even.

He barked out a laugh. "I'm afraid Monsieur Chevalier has declined our invitation to speak with us at the station. We are going to him." A slight French accent touched his lips when he spoke the French word and name, but otherwise he sounded like he'd been born and raised in the Midwest.

"And why are we interviewing a member of the Magister's family?"

"His son, Nicolas, worked with your first victim." He pulled the folder out from under his arm and flipped it open. "Claire Simons. Vasquez believes we need to interview him." Claude's tone left little doubt about his feelings on the subject.

"I take it you think we're wasting our time?"

"Were your victims missing a significant amount of blood? Did you find any bite marks?"

It wasn't a question, not really. He'd read the reports. "And you're stuck on this wild-goose chase because?" I asked.

"The Chevalier family has requested my presence."

Of course they had. Despite laws protecting them, vampires had suffered more than most species since all other-worlders had been forced to come out into the public eye, because of all the new scientific advances—particularly in forensics. They were dead, after all, and powerful. Both of those traits scared people. Oh, they'd concealed how powerful they really were when they revealed themselves to humanity, and continued to do so, I suspected. It was understandable that the Chevaliers would want a vampire police officer present during any questioning. And Claude was the highest-ranking vampire on the force.

"All right, then. Let's get this done." I downed the rest of the coffee, happy to find it had cooled a bit during our discussion. The dark liquid had the perfect amount of sugar. Trust Claude to remember such a small detail.

I followed him, shrugging away his offer to give me a ride in his shiny new hot rod. I didn't want to linger at the Chevalier house or end up stuck with another to-do from the lieutenant when we got back to the station. I had my own priorities. Ones that didn't involve catering to Vasquez's pet prejudices.

• • •

I followed Claude to an estate tucked into a close suburb. It was near the forest preserve and mostly out of sight behind vegetation cleverly planted to hide a tall fence running the full length of the property. The gloomy morning fit the place, or maybe it only seemed to because of the occupants. I'd been to the Magister's home only once before, although I hadn't met the Magister himself. Amanda and I had accompanied Claude and his partner—the unit's sensitive, Astrid—to arrest a young vampire for murder. The Magister himself informed the police, and his people held the murderer until we arrived.

But that murderer hadn't been a member of Lucas Chevalier's family.

The heavy smell of unshed rain and the sound of cicadas filled the air as we walked up to the large double doors in the front of what could only be called a mansion. Large block stonework formed imposing walls to create a building that looked hundreds of years older than it could have been. Columns—some architectural features, others standing firm to hold large eaves—lined the structure. The columns and building were a light grayish color, with just a hint of cream to the tone. Tall windows were sectioned off by pieces of metal that formed geometric designs with the glass. Standing proudly on balconies and at the dark gray rooftop were small statues of indiscernible people in flowing robes. It was so grand and unfamiliar, it had to be a style Chevalier had brought with him from France.

Claude walked up to me and opened his mouth to speak, but he stopped when a Jeep rolled down the driveway behind us.

My stomach dropped. I recognized that Jeep.

Aidan parked next to my Rav4 and stepped out of his car. His dark hair and jacket matched the gloomy setting. And for that matter, my mood.

"Did you follow us here?" I asked, pushing down my sudden urge to smile at him like an idiot. I was not happy to see him, dammit.

"I'm helping, remember? And I was coming to the

station to talk to you and saw you head out. I decided to follow." He held his hand to Claude and the vampire shook it.

"This is Aidan from the OWEA," I explained. "He's investigating the murders too, but it's kind of off the radar."

"Agent." Claude nodded to Aidan. "Give us a sec, will
you?"

Claude tugged on my arm and I followed him across the
parking lot. Aidan scowled at us, but didn't follow. "Listen to
me, Mac. If anything happens in there…" He shot the building a quick glance. "I need you to stick close to me. Vampires
can be…testy when challenged. And territorial."

I frowned. He wasn't telling me anything I didn't know,
even if it wasn't first hand knowledge.

Claude returned my frown with a serious look, not an
expression I was used to seeing on the vampire's face. "If
anything happens, if anyone crosses a line, you need to stick
by me. I'll get you out safely."

"Why are you telling me this? Making promises that
could get your ass in trouble?"

"You've defended me and mine more than once to Vasquez and those like him," he replied airily, his usual slightly
arrogant grin back on his face. "Besides, I've grown rather
fond of you the last couple of years."

I didn't know what to say to that so I just turned on my
heel and walked up to the door, leaving Claude and Aidan
to follow.

The doors opened before we got close enough to knock,
and an honest-to-goodness butler—an aged man complete
with suit—admitted us with a nod to Claude. We followed
the butler to a small office not far from the front entrance.
I tried not to gape at the tall built-in bookcases, impressive

mahogany furniture, and antique lamps while we waited for our host.

"Do your best to be polite," Claude said to me, back stiff in the formal chair.

I opened my mouth to tell him I was always polite, thank you very much, but the door behind us unlatched before the words could pass my lips.

The man who strolled in didn't look like a vampire, let alone one strong enough to hold an entire city the size of Chicago. And the unassuming young-looking man with the dark hair and a slightly too-wide nose especially didn't look strong enough to control all of the vampires in three states. He wasn't particularly tall—maybe five feet nine inches. A square jaw and dark brown eyes added to his average appearance. No power rolled off of him, seeking to overwhelm me, no supernatural aura of fear made my heart race around him. If I didn't know who he was, I would have dismissed him as nothing but a normal young man.

I would have been wrong.

Claude bowed his head to the Magister as he rounded the desk. He walked behind it, looking out of place among the old things surrounding him. After a quick jerk of his head to Claude, his attention moved to Aidan. He nodded to him as well, a contemplative expression on his face, and then he turned to look at me.

"This is Detective McLoughlin. Mac, this is Lucas Chevalier, Magister of the Northern Midwest Territory," Claude said. "This is Aidan Byrne. He's assisting with the investigation."

"Mr. Chevalier," I said.

"Please, call me Luc." He smiled at me, and I wiped my palms on my pants, but he didn't move to shake my hand.

Throat suddenly dry, I didn't offer to shake his either.

I gave him a quick nod when I couldn't think of the right response and turned my attention to Claude. His eyes never left the other vampire.

"Detective, thank you for agreeing to see my son here rather than at your police station." Luc sat down, seeming at ease with police in his house.

"Not sure it was much of a choice, but you're welcome."

Luc Chevalier laughed, and motioned toward the doorway. A man who bore a striking resemblance to the Magister strode into the room, assessing Claude and me before quickly dismissing us and looking at his father. They could have been brothers, and I wondered if they were actually blood relatives. Such a thing wasn't unthinkable, but it would mean that Nicolas was nearly as old as Luc. Could he be his actual son? If so, it meant Luc had fathered him before going through the change, as they called it. Vampires were not alive, and therefore couldn't biologically father children.

"This is my son, Nicolas. He will answer your questions."

Nicolas leaned against the desk rather than sitting in one of the extra chairs dotted around the room, and crossed his arms. Unlike Claude and Lucas, a clear feeling of something wrong rolled off of this vampire, with a touch of the fear their race was known to cause in humans and otherworlders alike. Like the sex appeal of succubi, it wasn't something they could control. Not according to common knowledge, anyway. I shot a quick glance at Claude. I'd always assumed that the stronger the vampire, the more aggressive the aura of fear that followed him. Stuck in a room with one of the most powerful vampires in the city—a man who seemed to elicit no fear whatsoever—made me wonder if the opposite was true.

"I understand you worked with Claire Simons?" I asked, pulling out a small notepad and pen from my pocket.

He shrugged. "I guess you could say that. I'm an attorney. She was a paralegal. She didn't even work on my cases."

"Did you know her outside of the office?"

"She wasn't exactly my type."

"Really? That's not what I heard." I'd heard no such thing, but I hoped the rumor that vampires could tell if the living lied was a fairy tale, or at least an exaggeration.

Luc Chevalier's chin rose slightly, and he stared at his son. I couldn't see a change in his expression, but the sneer faded from Nicolas's face and he uncrossed his arms.

"Look, I didn't associate with her outside of work. I didn't even really notice her. She just didn't hit my radar," he said, tone matter-of-fact.

"Oh really? Why is that? She didn't look tasty enough for you?"

His lip drew back in a snarl. "I wouldn't say that. All you humans taste pretty much the same to me."

"Watch who you're calling human, Fang."

Nicolas knelt in front of me, face only inches from mine, in less time than it took me to blink. His wide mouth revealed the very things I'd used to insult him, and he hissed, the sound escaping between his fangs as naturally as it would a snake.

A second later he was back across the room, held against the wall several inches off the floor, secured by Claude's forearm under his neck. Aidan stood between them and me, his attention focused on Nicolas. His hands were clenched tightly at his sides and he stood in a fighter's stance, legs wide set.

The hissing Nicolas had started at me continued, but it was now directed at his assailant. Spittle flew from his lips onto Claude's face and neck and I flinched in disgust. Disgust was easier to deal with than the fear making my heart pound incessantly in my chest.

Luc Chevalier didn't move from his chair, but when he spoke it was as if the air had left the room. "Nicolas, you will behave yourself or face the consequences. Claude, release him. We will discuss why you feel you can manhandle my family later." He turned his gaze to me and for a brief moment I felt the power he kept hidden. Only a glimpse, but it was enough to make me vow then and there to stay the hell away from vampires if I could—this vampire especially.

Aidan moved to my side and gripped my shoulder, just for a moment. Something about his steadiness next to me settled my fear. I forced myself to ask a few more pointed questions designed to get another rise out of Nicolas, but he didn't go for the bait. I couldn't shake the feeling there was something off about Nicolas Chevalier, but nothing seemed to tie him to this case. I wasn't going to poke around in a hopeless effort to figure out what it was about him that my subconscious didn't like. Suicide wasn't on my to-do list.

A short time later, we were escorted from the office to the front door, and sent on our way. I searched my memory for the exact effect my screams would have on vampires, but couldn't recall anything specific outside of mild discomfort. I made a mental note to research the effect of banshee screams on the bloodsuckers the second I got home. I was pretty sure they would be even less effective than on humans, but couldn't hurt to be certain.

"Sorry your time was wasted out here," Claude said as we reached our cars.

I stopped in my tracks. He was really going to act like nothing unusual had happened in there? Fine. He'd helped me, so I'd pretend if it made him feel better. Besides, I needed to get the hell out of this place. I had to make sure Amanda was okay. She hadn't checked in with me for too long. I didn't have time to waste on bullshit like telling Claude Desmarais exactly what I thought of his kind and his Magister. I shrugged. "Not your fault. Vasquez…thought this was a good lead," I finished lamely.

"Besides," Aidan said, "I wouldn't say it was a total waste. Hell, it was worth it for me to watch you knock that guy down a peg."

Claude laughed, and then got in his car and waved. The roar of his engine interrupted the otherwise relatively silent day. Only the sound of cicadas filled the silence when he got far enough away that I was able to hear anything but his car again.

"I've got to go," I told Aidan. "I'll see you later, okay?"

He nodded, but his eyes followed me as I jumped into my SUV. I glanced at my cell phone while I pulled on the seat belt, which kept my eyes firmly away from the sexy man I really wanted to stare at. No missed calls. Giving the vampire's opulent lair one last fearful glance, I headed back down the long driveway.

• • •

Amanda's house sat surrounded by mature trees and a sprawling lawn in an older neighborhood full of large lots that offered ample privacy. It was a small home, painted a medium blue with white shutters that were never closed. Bright daisies had overtaken the area between the house and yard. Only the concrete steps leading to the front door hadn't been overwhelmed by the aggressive, cheerful flower.

The tightly locked front door barred my entry. I banged on it a few times before peering through the window, pushing down my panic. It just wasn't like her to go so long without contacting me—or at least Vasquez. But her house looked like it was in order. No bloody handprints on the wall, no knocked over knick knacks, no furniture pushed from its normal spot on the floor. I took a deep breath, told myself there was no real reason to worry, and headed to the back. The knob was also locked. I knocked twice. No answer. I took my driver's license out of my wallet.

As a cop, Amanda knew to keep deadbolts on all of her doors. But she'd just moved into this house and she hadn't had time to add them to the older home. Slipping the license between the door and the frame, I jiggled it and pushed. A few seconds later it popped open, revealing Amanda's tidy kitchen. Like her locks, it also needed some updating, but it oozed charm, with checkerboard tile flooring and white cabinets. No dishwasher, but like me, she lived alone so the dishes weren't too much of a burden.

She'd given a housewarming party the week after she'd moved in. A crazy organizer, she'd unpacked every box, hung every picture, before the party. It was a cop party. Nearly everyone Amanda knew was a cop. She didn't have any family to speak of, so we were the only ones she invited. Entertainment had been limited to the Bears game on her small television, and visiting with other guests and the hostess. But she'd supplied us with a lot of beer and food, which was enough to keep a bunch of cops and their families happy.

I stepped through the kitchen into her formal dining room. I secretly thought this was the reason Amanda bought the house. Spacious enough to hold the antique table her mother left her when she passed, it was a room meant to be used by a large family. Despite her normally dismissive attitude on the subject, Amanda dreamed of having a big family someday, a secret she'd confided in me one night after too many drinks.

Two place settings sat on the dining room table, with one plate practically licked clean and the other with small chunks of mashed potatoes and a couple of green beans still on it. Wine glasses—both empty—sat behind the plates. Two candles with blackened wicks sat on the middle of the table. The food looked like it had been there since the night before: crusty, but with no sign of mold.

Sudden pressure on my chest suffocated me and perspiration covered my face. Amanda was meticulous with everything in her life. She would never leave dirty dishes lying around. I wiped a sweaty palm on my jeans and moved slowly toward her bedroom.

I almost turned and walked away when the subtle smell touched my nose. Calling in backup wouldn't make me less of a cop. I was only human—well, mostly. But if she weren't behind the door, I'd never live it down. I tried to tell myself that the scent came from the dirty dishes in the dining room. Although every cell in my body screamed my worst nightmare waited for me, I couldn't turn away. I didn't want to remember her how I would almost certainly find her behind that door. I needed to remember her for her dry sense of humor, her tireless devotion to duty, her loyalty to her friends and fellow cops, and her willingness to befriend a half-assed member of a species so dangerous they couldn't live among normal humans.

I twisted the doorknob, pulling out my gun as the door creaked open.

Amanda lay on her bed, eyes clouded and wide-open, head hanging off the foot of the bed so she stared at the door. Her limp hair streamed down, almost touching the carpet. Lipstick still colored her mouth, and mascara smudged under her eyes. Gritting my teeth and swallowing a scream, I turned from her and went to call it in.

My partner was dead.

Chapter Four

I hadn't felt the urge to scream so badly in a very long time. Not because any vision of death struck me, but because I'd just seen my worst nightmare. I wanted to yell and curse and scream because it hurt so much. Only the thought of how pissed Amanda would be if I broke the windows in her new house prevented me from wailing my heart out. So instead of howling, I sat on a chair next to the door in her bedroom and waited for everyone to arrive. I didn't touch her. The cloudiness in her still-open eyes kept me from an inane hope she might still be alive. She would be cold. I didn't want to remember my friend as cold.

By the time the crews of emergency personnel circulated through and my boss arrived, I had regained some semblance of control. Lieutenant Vasquez stared down at me, blocking my view of Amanda. His eyes were tight, and his mouth formed a grim line.

"Let's go talk in the kitchen." His tone brooked no

argument, and he headed out of the bedroom without waiting for me to get up.

I rose from the chair, feeling my legs protest. My backside was numb and I vaguely wondered how long I'd been sitting. I glanced one last time at Amanda, and then walked out to her kitchen.

The lieutenant stood, arms crossed, next to the sink. A frown creased his face. It was as close to upset as his expression ever got.

I pulled one of the chairs from her small breakfast table and sat down heavily. The grief that had pressed on my chest was gone, and the realization that one of the only people I'd thought of as a friend was now dead remained distant. I was numb. On some level, I realized my numbness was due to shock, but my mind shied from studying my emotions too closely.

"Tell me."

"I hadn't been able to get ahold of her since Monday night, at the Rebecca Anderson murder scene. She left me a voice mail with some instructions, said she was going to be out of touch for a bit. When you told me you hadn't heard from her either…" I waited for the rebuke, for him to say I should have said something this morning, not come over here by myself.

"Go on," he said.

"House was locked tight. I broke in the back door. She hadn't had time to install a dead bolt."

"You get any other info yet on the earlier victims, the ones outside our jurisdiction?"

"No. I haven't gotten them from my OWEA contact." Belatedly I remembered promising Aidan I wouldn't mention the OWEA's involvement to anyone. Oh, well—not like

I could keep that to myself now anyway. A dead cop upped the stakes for Lieutenant Vasquez. Amanda's death changed everything for me.

"OWEA's involved?"

"Yeah, not…officially, though."

A flicker of emotion flashed across his face. Annoyance, maybe. But before I could identify it, the expression disappeared. "What's the agent's name?"

"Byrne. Aidan Byrne."

He jotted the name down on a small pad of paper. "Anything else I need to know?"

"I've told you everything, Lieutenant."

"Good." He nodded, and then hesitated before he said, "Can you get yourself home? I could tell a uniform to—"

"Home? I'm not going home." The numbness abruptly disappeared and a burning hole ate at the middle of my chest. I could either cry in front of my lieutenant or be pissed off at him. Given the choice, I'll always go with angry over sad.

"Of course you're going home. Your partner was murdered for Christ's sake." He crossed his arms and looked down at me like I was slightly daft.

"Screw that! I just needed a…breather. I'm fine. I'm helping. No way in hell am I going home." I glared at him and he stared back at me, irritation plain on his face.

"You're no longer on this case, Mac. You're going home."

"That's bullsh—"

"Shut it! I understand how you feel right now, but this isn't a discussion. You'll go home under your own power, or I will have someone escort you. Is that clear?" His eyelid twitched. Lieutenant Vasquez did not run a democracy, and his officers arguing with him when he'd made up his mind was one of the few things that pissed him off.

I opened my mouth to protest, and then snapped it shut. Squabbling with the lieutenant wouldn't get me anywhere. "Fine," I said, keeping my voice even. "But I'd appreciate it if you'd keep me informed." *That's the least you can do, jerk.*

He gave me a quick nod and pointed at the door, his message clear.

The door clicked shut behind me and I was proud of myself for not slamming it. I was a freaking professional.

The burning ember at the end of a cigarette caught my eye. I met Mason Sanderson's hard gaze with one of my own. The night hid his features, but I recognized him even in the low light. The Internal Affairs cop didn't say anything.

Even though Mason stood outside of the building, leaning against a tall, old tree, I had the uneasy feeling that he had heard my exchange with Vasquez. I didn't need Internal Affairs on my ass, so I held my tongue. A couple of seconds into our staring contest, he nodded at me, his expression solemn. I nodded back, unable to speak, and headed for my car.

I probably hadn't convinced the lieutenant I was going to follow his orders to a T, at least not for long, but he almost certainly figured he'd cowed me for the short-term. I smiled. He didn't know me that well.

What he didn't know couldn't hurt me.

• • •

I considered heading to my dad's house instead of home. It would take over an hour—he lived in a town so far out it could hardly be called a suburb. The drive would be worth it to get a big bear hug from him and the reassurance that

everything was going to be okay. But along with the reassur-
ances, I'd have to deal with the subtle hints that this wasn't
the best line of work for me to be in, and the less-than-subtle
statements from my stepmother to that effect. I loved them,
and they were great parents, but they couldn't accept the
fact I was a cop. Neither of them liked that my job put me in
danger, or that my freak squad status constantly reminded
them I wasn't entirely human. Both of them were human,
and while it wasn't a fact they held against me consciously, I
knew it lingered in the back of their minds.

The numbness returned by the time I turned into my
neighborhood. The world felt surreal. Lights were too bright,
colors bled dry of their brilliance. Pulling into my driveway,
I smashed my foot on the brakes to avoid hitting the Jeep
already parked there. As my car jarred to a stop, I heard a
crunch. I jammed down on the clutch, and threw my Rav4
into reverse and backed up enough to check the damage.

I slammed the car door and walked up between the
cars. A small dent bent my bumper in. The Jeep had a single
scratch. A light shone from inside my house, stealing some
of the night away and casting long shadows in the driveway.
Eyes narrowing, I stomped up to the front porch. I swung the
door open, cringing as it hit the wall with a loud thump. If
that left a mark on my wall, I was going to be doubly pissed.

I strode through the living room into the dining room.
Sure enough, he was there. Feet on my table, the same romance novel he had been perusing before in his hand, cup
of coffee steaming on the table in front of him. How did he
find where I hid the pile of books? Did he go through my
coat closet?

He looked up from my novel, dark blue eyes crinkling at

the edges, a hint of a smile on his handsome face. Suddenly, I was glad to see him. Yelling at Aidan sounded infinitely more appealing than crying my eyes out.

"You owe me a bumper." I tossed my files on the table and headed for the kitchen. No way was I asking about the book. Was he actually reading it? Grabbing a cup out of the cabinet, I poured the coffee and struggled to keep my voice even. "We have a new victim."

"You're sure it's the same killer?"

I walked into the dining room and sat down at the table, in front of where I'd thrown the files. I took a sip of my coffee before I spoke, considering how much to tell him. Since I was officially off the case and he might be my only chance of getting in on the latest information, I decided to spill.

"Yes. Same M.O." I hesitated, and then forced out the rest between gritted teeth. "Vic was my partner, Amanda Franklin." I concentrated very hard on my coffee cup. If I glimpsed pity in his eyes, I'd go over the edge into either tears or a fit of rage. Neither would help me find her killer.

Silence filled the air for a long moment. Finally he said, "We're going to get this asshole, Kiera. We'll get him and nail him to the wall."

I risked a glance up from my coffee cup. No pity adorned his face, but the half smile he always wore was gone. His calm expression belied a hardness in his eyes that I hadn't seen in him before. For a split second they looked almost inhuman, but then the crazy edge disappeared and only the cold rage remained.

It suddenly struck me that Aidan Byrne might be more than just a pretty face.

"I've been tossed from the investigation."

His hint of a smile reappeared. "And I'm technically not on this case at all. Sounds like we make quite the pair."

Investigating a case I was emotionally involved in with a man who was more than attractive sounded like a bad idea. Unfortunately, it was my best shot at finding Amanda's killer—maybe my only shot now that I'd pissed off Lieutenant Vasquez.

"Fine. We'll work together on this one. But that doesn't make us friends, and it doesn't mean I trust you as far as I can throw you." I leaned across the table and gave him my best cop face. "And no funny business."

His grin turned into a full-on smile, revealing a set of sparkling white, perfect teeth. "Oh, I can keep my hands to myself if you can."

I snapped my mouth shut when I realized I was gaping at him while he disappeared into the kitchen with his coffee cup. When he reappeared in the dining room, I'd managed to put my blank face back on.

When you're without a good comeback, ignore, ignore, ignore. "So we're looking for an incubus. Possibly a succubus impersonating one, but I think that's less likely."

"Incubi have been extinct for over one hundred years."

"I'm aware of that. But, it's the only explanation that works. Not only does it fit, it fits like a freaking puzzle piece."

"Except for the fact that not only are they extinct, they've also never been known for killing their food."

"Killers come in all shapes and sizes, Aidan. There's nothing about incubi that I've ever heard of that prevents them from killing. Our sensitive confirmed at least one of our victims was drained of her psychic energy. The method fits, the sex fits, the fact they all died without a struggle fits.

It all fits."

"And you don't think it's more likely to be a succubus because?" he asked, his voice annoyingly calm and reasonable.

"Call it a gut instinct. Call it experience. Call it statistics. How many sex crime–related female serial killers have we seen in the last few decades?"

"Okay. Let's say it is an incubus. Why would he bother to kill his victims when he could feed on them—probably forever—without them complaining about it?"

"Using otherworlder powers to influence a person to do something is a felony. It's treated just like forcing someone with a gun." Why was I lecturing another cop on the justice system? I couldn't help myself. "That, on top of feeding from them, would net this guy some serious jail time."

"Yes, but the chances of women actually filing a complaint are almost nil…if incubi are like their succubi cousins, that is."

He was right. From what we knew of them, incubi were just as welcome by women as their cousins were welcome by men, which may have led to their extinction. Jealous husbands and all. A forced seduction charge didn't fit, especially for the victims who didn't have a significant other to complain about their change in behavior.

As he waited for my retort, I studied the man across from me. He was dressed casually, wearing a T-shirt and jeans. I could make out the muscles under his shirt. I imagined it would burst at the seams if he flexed. Not likely, but it was a conveniently distracting thought. My gaze made its way up to his face, where a small smile brought me out of my pondering. I frowned at him and he grinned more widely. Bastard knew exactly how attractive he was.

"Okay, then how about a motivation not directly incubi related?" Heat flooded my cheeks. If he said anything about my blushing, I would shoot him. "Maybe, like your garden-variety serial killer, he just enjoys killing people. Gets off on it. Might be he's a nutcase who just happens to be an incubus."

"Perhaps. But if that's true, how do we find him?"

"You any good at tracking spells?"

"I'm not a witch," he said.

"Just checking." I resisted the urge to stick my tongue out at him. "Guess we're going to have to rely on good old-fashioned police work."

"Considering the OWEA isn't officially working on the case, and you've been booted from it, how do you plan to do that?"

I winked at him, feeling silly the instant I did it. Forcing my embarrassment down I said, "I have my ways." Then, to fully cover my discomfort, I went on the offensive. "What kind of otherworlder are you, anyway?"

He frowned. "You just toss social propriety to the wind, don't you?" He thought about it for a second, and then said, "I'm a sex god. That's my special power."

Heat crept up into my cheeks again and I fled, walking quickly to the kitchen with a muttered excuse that I needed more coffee. It had been a rude question, and he had every right to deflect, but that didn't mean I didn't have the right to know. He might not tell me, but I'd figure it out. Aidan Byrne was hiding something.

I let the matter drop and we discussed the case until I could barely keep my eyes open. Then I pushed him out my door, ignoring his sexy grin and suggestion that he should stay to keep me company. After I moved my car from where it blocked his, I watched his Jeep disappear into the night, and I almost wished I'd taken him up on his offer. A night of fun, distracting sex might be just what the doctor ordered. It had been a long time, after all. A wave of loneliness hit me when I thought about how long since I'd had sex, let alone anything remotely approaching a real relationship.

Pushing thoughts of Aidan aside, I tried to force away the overwhelming desire to be held that had plagued me since I'd seen Amanda's body, and I hugged my pillow and cried.

How will I find the asshole who killed you without your help?

Chapter Five

After a few restless hours, I dragged myself out of bed and into the kitchen. The sun still hid well beyond the horizon, and would for hours yet. But I couldn't sleep. Not with Amanda's killer still loose, probably out looking for more victims.

Coffee brewing, I grabbed my laptop and logged in. A few passwords later I'd signed into the Illinois State Police Criminal Records Database. It wouldn't offer a complete search, but the national database was only accessible from behind the firewalls at the station.

I ran the first search on Marisol Whitfield, twinging a bit at running a search on a fellow cop. No records appeared, and a bit of tension released from my neck. But I wasn't done. Marisol had been hiding something. I was sure of it.

A search under Whitfield netted over a dozen names. I poured a cup of coffee before looking through them. I didn't recognize any, but one of the addresses tugged at my memory. The woman, Elaine Whitfield, lived on the south side of the city. Her criminal record had been sealed. She'd been tried as a minor. Accessing sealed records was beyond my pay grade.

Not only could I not access much of anything about Elaine Whitfield, I also couldn't access Marisol's address. But memory pulled at me, and I was fairly certain she lived in the same area as Elaine Whitfield. Moreover, Marisol had mentioned having a sister a time or two in casual conversation. I'd never caught the sister's name, but Elaine's date of birth put her a few years younger than me. Just in the right range to be Marisol's sister.

"Is that what you're hiding?" I muttered to myself.

Since the police database didn't offer specifics, I turned to Google. The Whitfield name turned up little, and none of it seemed specific to the Whitfields I was looking for.

"Dammit." I snapped the laptop shut. This was getting me nowhere. I needed real information. I might not be able to access sealed files, but I knew someone who could.

While I waited for Aidan to pick up the line, I fingered the plain white card. He answered on the second ring. "Byrne," he said, voice rough with sleep.

I glanced at the clock before I said anything and mentally winced at the time. "Hey, I need a favor." My voice came out steadier than I expected.

"Kiera?" He sounded confused. "Are you all right?"

"I'm fine." *Liar.* "I need you to pull a sealed court record for me."

Silence filled the line for ten agonizing seconds before he replied, and I tapped my pen nervously against the closed laptop. Finally he said, "Do I want to know what this is about?"

"Just following a hunch. Will you run her name or not?"

"What's the name?"

"Elaine Whitfield." I rattled off the address and he said he'd be in touch.

I turned back to the database and plugged in the next name I needed more info on. Aidan Byrne. A few seconds later, the computer spit out no information. Again, not surprising if he was a cop. The same search in Google netted info on a chef and a college athlete, as well as a few social website pages. Nothing relating to a cop or a criminal. I leaned back in the chair and crossed my arms. I'd bet my badge the man, distractingly hot as he was, and helpful as he seemed to be, was hiding something.

It felt like everyone was hiding something. I shook my head. The second thing Amanda taught me on the job. Paranoia is a cop's gift and curse.

My phone rang and I grabbed it and flipped it open. "Find anything?"

"First of all, you're welcome." Aidan still sounded groggy. To me it sounded like sexy, just-woke-up-after-a-night-of-amazing-sex groggy. Dammit. "And you won't believe what I found."

• • •

Marisol Whitfield and her sister, Elaine, lived in a small row-style home in the southern part of the city. I found parking a block away and stalked up to the house. The sun peeked over the horizon, and while it was still well shy of what most would consider a decent hour, I didn't care.

I hit the bell and then rapped on the door. After a few seconds I sounded the bell again, and it opened to reveal a bleary-eyed Marisol.

"What's going on, Mac? Something wrong? I didn't get a call." She stepped back from the door and glanced down at the cell phone she held in her hand. Her short, silky nightgown and matching robe fit her. And I was irritated to see that while she wore no makeup, she didn't seem any less attractive.

I stepped into the house and she looked up from her phone, frowning.

"What's this about?" Marisol asked.

"Mari? Is everything all right?" A young woman who looked like she was in her early twenties stood at the top of the stairs. She wore a T-shirt and cotton shorts, and her resemblance to her sister was unmistakable.

"It's fine. Go back to bed. It's a work thing," Marisol said.

I opened my mouth to argue but Marisol shot me a glare. Her sister nodded and disappeared back down the hallway.

"Why are you here, Mac?" she hissed.

"I'm here to find out why you lied to me."

"Lied to you? What are you talking about?"

"I'm talking about the fact that you not only knew Rebecca could have been killed by a succubus, but you knew of a succubus who has killed before and kept it from me."

"Keep your voice down." She shot a glance upstairs. "Let's talk in the other room."

I followed Marisol to the kitchen, and she waved me to a seat at a small breakfast table. She started a kettle of water on the stove.

"I'm sorry," she said, sitting down at the table while the water heated. "I probably should have said something, but I didn't want her dragged into this. How much do you know?"

"Elaine was charged with mystical manslaughter when she was sixteen years old. The charges were dropped and the records were sealed because of her age." Mystical manslaughter carried a sentence closer to that of second-degree murder than it did regular voluntary manslaughter. It was a double standard, but otherworlders with lethal powers were held to a higher standard. Fear and politics kept the law on the books—in most states, anyway.

Marisol let out a long breath. "Okay, I see why you might jump to conclusions. But you had no right to come here." Her eyes narrowed. "How did you find out? Unless you got a promotion or two since yesterday, there's no way you could have accessed those records."

"How I got the records isn't important."

"Oh, it's important. Was it Vasquez? That ass—"

"Amanda's dead."

Marisol's eyes widened. The teapot whistled and, when Marisol made no move to retrieve it, I got up and pulled the ceramic pot from the burner. I shut off the stove and turned to face her.

I didn't want to see her sympathy, her sadness. But Marisol either wasn't as adept as most cops at keeping her emotions from her face, or she didn't bother employing that skill. Her eyes filled with unshed tears, and she wrapped her arms around herself.

"Was it the serial killer you're hunting?"

I nodded, not trusting myself to speak, and then turned and started opening cupboards at random. I found the tea first and the cups two doors later. I poured tea, setting one cup in front of Marisol before sitting back down.

She didn't seem to see the tea. "I'll tell you what happened with my sister so you can take her off the list."

"Okay," I said, voice rough. I swallowed the lump in my throat and tried again. "What happened?"

"Elaine was attacked by an older kid at school when she was sixteen. He was eighteen. They'd gone out a couple of times. She didn't know he'd found out she was a succubus until it was too late. When he did, he figured a succubus should always be willing to put out. Pissed off she wouldn't sleep with him, he raped her."

I closed my eyes. "I'm so sorry, Marisol."

"Do you know how succubi powers work?"

I opened my eyes and blinked a couple of times to clear them. "Not really. I mean, I know you can drain the life force from people."

Marisol nodded slowly. "But when we use our powers, it's kind of a sharing process. We can get bits of emotion from the other person. How they're feeling. It builds a connection. The more drained, the closer a connection is built."

"Wouldn't that make it hard? To date, I mean?"

She gave me a tight smile. "We don't have to drain people. We aren't vampires. Succubi are sustained just fine with the five food groups. Draining can give power, but most succubi don't use their powers until they're in a long-term relationship. Married, usually. It can make the couple closer. The connection works both ways, you know? The succubus gains energy and a connection, and her lover gains pieces of her, too."

"Does the effect...fade?"

Marisol took a sip of her tea, and then shook her head. "Elaine lost control. She was so scared. She thought he was going to kill her. And he may very well have, but she drained him first. I'm not even certain she knew what she was doing. She just wanted him to stop."

I grimaced and tried to push out of my head the fear the poor child had probably felt. I had to stay focused. "So will the connection—"

"She'll always have part of him in her head. Always feel him. His anger, his lust, his hatred of her." She wiped at the tears that had started to trail down her cheeks, and then took a deep breath. "But it'll get better. She's already improved. A couple more years…maybe she'll be ready to think about building a life for herself. A real life."

An image of Marisol taking care of her pretty young sister, a shut-in with God knew what kind of emotional problems, flashed in my mind.

And I had thought her shallow.

"Marisol, I—" I choked on the words.

She shook her head and reached across the table to take my hand. "Hush, Mac. What's done is done. What you need to worry about now is finding Amanda's killer."

I took a few deep breaths, and when I was sure I could speak without the threat of tears, I said, "Vasquez has taken me off the case. Says I'm too close."

"I'm sure he's right." She grinned, face still damp from her tears. "I'm also sure that won't stop you. How can I help?"

"Do you think this is a succubus or an incubus?"

She nodded. "Could be either. I know incubi are commonly thought of as extinct, but after reading the files and looking at the body, I think that's what the killer has to be.

Sure, it could be a succubus, but that's a reach."

"And an extinct species isn't?" I swallowed another mouthful of tea, wishing it were coffee.

She laughed. "Well, there have been rumors that incubi aren't extinct, just very rare."

"And you've heard these rumors where?"

"They're our cousins, almost the same species, really. I've heard it around from other succubi."

"Jesus Christ," I said. "Don't tell Vasquez that. It'll confirm his fucking conspiracy theories."

I finished my tea and then Marisol showed me out. As she shut her door firmly behind me, my cell phone rang. The number flashing on the screen made me sigh, but I flipped it open.

"Yes?"

"Is that the kind of tone you use for someone who just helped you get sealed information?" Aidan asked.

I rubbed my temple with my free hand. "That's the kind of tone I use for someone who thinks he needs to check up on me all the damn time."

He laughed. "Did you find anything on the succubus?"

"Nothing relevant."

"So what are you going to do now?"

That was a damn good question.

• • •

After leaving Marisol's house I returned home to plan. I knew what I needed, but I wasn't sure who to call. Marisol would do what she could for me. Claude probably would, too. But they both reported to Vasquez, and helping me would put their careers at risk. That wasn't something I was willing to do. Luckily, I knew one person who might be able to come to my aid. And he wasn't under Vasquez's jurisdiction.

Gathering favors seemed to be the only political skill I'd acquired in my time as a cop. Any ability to kiss ass or even not rub people the wrong way proved beyond me. As such, I was fairly certain I'd never rise above my current position as a detective and that was A-OK with me. The idea of being stuck in an office all day every day was my own personal version of hell.

"Agrusa," said a deep voice on the other end of the phone line.

"Aggie. It's Mac."

"Mac, to what do I owe this pleasure?" he said, carefully.

"I need a favor." I tapped a pen on my kitchen table then realized he might hear it and stopped. I didn't want him to think I was nervous. One moment of weakness and he'd know he could get out of this.

"This doesn't have anything to do with a certain investigation you're no longer part of, does it?"

Crap. Word was already out. Ignoring his question, I said, "I need you to get me a copy of a file."

"What file?" he asked. I figured the question was rhetorical, or at the very least, pointless, but I answered it anyway.

"Amanda Franklin's."

Aggie cursed under his breath. "It's a cop's file, Mac. It's going to be damned difficult to gain access to it, let alone get a copy out of the building."

"I know that, but she was my partner, Aggie. I need the fucking file."

"I'm not even on the freak squad. Why don't you call

one of your coworkers?"

"I know you can do it, Aggie, and you don't report to Vasquez." The lieutenant would be hard-pressed to make him pay in any kind of significant way, even if he did find out Aggie passed the file along to me. Most people on the squad who weren't closet or openly otherworlders landed there because they'd screwed up or pissed off someone important. When weird shit went down we were called in, and left to it, but no one was happy to see us otherwise. Aggie's boss wouldn't give him shit if Vasquez made a stink about him helping me, and Aggie knew it.

There was silence on the other end of the line.

"You owe me, Aggie." It had been almost five years since I'd let Aggie talk me out of an arrest that would have forever tainted his oldest daughter's record. I'd been a uniform then, and only a couple of years with my badge. Truth be told, I'd been more than a bit in awe of the homicide detective and had dropped the matter with a warning out of one part fear and two parts respect. But I'd changed over the years, and I wasn't afraid to cash in the favor.

He let out the breath he must have been holding for the last twenty seconds and muttered something noncommittal before the line clicked dead. I went to make another pot of coffee. I wasn't worried about Aggie coming through. He was a good man and a damn fine cop. And he owed me.

Two hours and three-quarters of a pot of coffee later, my doorbell rang. I trotted to the door, and then checked the peephole before opening it.

"Here," Aggie said, thrusting a thick file into my face. "It's what I could get. I'll let you know if I hear anything else." He paused, and an odd look flashed on his face, like he'd smelled something bad. "How are you?"

"Fine. Thanks."

"Good." He cleared his throat and shifted on his feet. "Well then." With those charming words of support, he turned on his heel and walked down the sidewalk, heading back to his car.

I shut the door behind him, flinching as it slammed, nose already in the copy of the file he'd brought me. They'd worked fast. An initial summary of her activities for the last few days had already been compiled, though there were a lot of blanks. Credit card activity for the last thirty days had been pulled. Aggie had even managed to snag the initial scene notes from the lead detective on the case.

The name made me grimace. Corey Williams. Like Vasquez, Williams was a normal on the freak squad because he'd pissed someone off. He took it personally, and didn't like associating with freaks.

The oak chair creaked faintly as I sat down at the table. I steeled myself to look through the file. Blinking back tears, I checked the initial Medical Examiner's report. I took a deep breath and swallowed a lump in my throat as I read through the sparse information. She'd been reduced to a victim: female, thirty-five years old, five feet eleven inches tall, single, no children. As a cop I had to keep my distance from victims. If I pondered the fact that the victims I examined with cold detachment were real people with lives that had come to an abrupt halt, it would make me crazy. But Amanda was real to me. Keeping my distance in this case was not an option.

A loud knock sounded from the door and I started. Had Aggie forgotten to give me something? I trotted back to the door and swung it open without checking the peephole.

Aidan stood on my step, a tight smile touching his lips.

Before I could open my mouth to tell him to go away, he said, "I'm here to help."

I swallowed hard and nodded.

He followed me to the dining room and glanced at the small stacks of papers that held the documents from Amanda's file. "So what do we have so far?"

I ignored the small skip my heart gave at his choice of words and said, "Not sure yet, I was just getting ready to go through her credit card and bank statements."

I pulled out the stack of credit-card bills, and passed half to Aidan. The Visa's last activity was two weeks prior to Amanda's death, at Nordstrom. The Discover card hadn't been used at all in the last month. Her bank statements were tucked in between her Visa and Discover lists. The last purchase was on the day of her death, for twelve dollars at The Grill House.

I cursed under my breath. "Got something," I said to Aidan.

How soon after I'd bantered back and forth with Aidan had she arrived? Hours? Less? If I'd lingered a few minutes longer, could I have saved her?

Chapter Six

Aidan followed me to The Grill House, and we went into the restaurant together. A new aura seemed to emanate from the diner. Normally welcoming, it felt faintly off to me as I walked through the front door. Nothing was actually different in the air—not being a sensitive I wouldn't have known it if there was. But it seemed off, knowing this was the last place Amanda showed up on the grid. According to her bank statement, she'd eaten an early dinner here, only four hours after my inadvertent lunch date with Aidan Byrne. The day she stood me up with the briefest of explanations.

I fought the urge to look at Aidan, but finally lost. His eyes were serious, but he offered me a small smile. My heart jumped, and I found myself smiling back.

"Table for two?" a voice asked.

"Lisa here?" I asked the hostess, pulling my gaze from Aidan. She'd gone from auburn hair to an almost white-colored bleached blonde. Between that and her pale skin, she looked like she'd disappear in a good snowstorm.

"Yeah, one sec."

She reappeared with Lisa in tow less than a minute later. Lisa's hair was still blue and spiky, but by next week I was betting it would be red or orange. Maybe green.

"Hi, Mac," she said, with a big customer-service smile plastered on her face. "And hello to you, too," she practically purred at Aidan, and I barely resisted the urge to smack them both.

"Lisa." I pulled her toward the entrance, away from the hostess who was leaning in to hear our conversation. "Can we talk?"

"Um…okay, I guess."

I headed outside, and Lisa shuffled behind me. Aidan held the door for us. He didn't seem to notice Lisa's longing gaze, but I did. Who did she think she was, anyway?

Not that I had any claim on him.

I took a deep breath and cleared my thoughts. As the door swung shut, the cool afternoon air touched my bare arms. Fall was definitely here. Lisa dragged her gaze from Aidan and looked at me, waiting for me to speak.

"Has anyone been here to talk to you?" Seeing her confused expression I added, "From the police?"

"About what?"

I took a deep breath. "Amanda's dead, Lisa."

"Amanda? Your partner?"

I nodded. Then looked away from the pity that flashed on her face.

"Oh, I'm so sorry, Mac." She gave me a quick, awkward hug. Her expression was now tinged with sadness, but the uncertainty was still there.

"Do you remember when I was here last Monday for lunch?"

"Oh, sure I do." She smiled and glanced at Aidan.

Of course she'd remember me coming in on Monday, since Aidan had joined me for lunch. I suppressed the glare I wanted to give her. I needed information and scaring her wasn't likely to help her memory.

"Did you see Amanda come in that night?"

"Yeah, I remember. She came in super late for your lunch date. I told her you'd been in earlier and it seemed like she didn't remember that she was supposed to meet you. She seemed…"

"What?"

"Confused, I guess. But happy, like, really happy. Ready to jump on a table and dance happy."

I frowned. Amanda was solid, and rarely showed her emotions. That kind of display wasn't like her. "Was she alone?"

"Yeah, but she was dressed up in a clubbing outfit. I asked her if she had a hot date and she said yes. Guess she was meeting him at Sylvester's." Lisa's eyes widened. "Do you think her date killed her? Oh my God!"

I ground my teeth together and forced out what I hoped was an encouraging smile. From the look on Lisa's face, I wasn't entirely successful but it was the best I could do.

"We don't know anything for sure yet. Can you think of anything else she might have said or done?" Aidan asked.

She shook her head. "No, sorry. I wish I did. She was a nice lady."

After quizzing Lisa for the next hour, making her walk me through Amanda's visit to the restaurant twice from start to finish, I decided she probably didn't know anything other than what she'd told me initially. Amanda had stopped in for a quick bite to eat on her way to a club to meet a man, she was elated—giddy even—and had seemed disoriented.

"Thanks for your help, Lisa," I said, already lost in thought. I gave her a quick wave, ignoring her questions, and stalked back to my Toyota. Annoyingly, Aidan lingered. Probably to smooth things over with the waitress, but I wasn't in any mood to be charitable about his intentions.

"Are you coming?" I called over my shoulder to Aidan. Without waiting for his reply, I opened my door and jumped in.

Aidan followed me as I drove to Sylvester's. Anger built in my chest. When had Amanda fallen under the incubus's thrall? It had to have been after I'd seen her at the crime scene, and after we played phone tag. I would have noticed if she'd been off her game. Wouldn't I? I shook my head in an attempt to rid myself of the small bit of doubt nagging me. Doubts were useless now. I had to concentrate on finding the asshole who had killed her.

It had to be an incubus—maybe a succubus. Everything fit. Succubi thralled their victims, pulling them into a dream-like state that lasted for hours, even days, which made their prey more pliable and easily influenced. Incubi could likely do the same thing. Records indicated their powers had been nearly identical to that of their succubi cousins. Marisol had confirmed that research, with what was as close to firsthand experience as I was going to get. Lisa hadn't seen the killer, but between her and Jason's statements, I was almost certain it was a man.

But why would the incubus let her out of his sight after he thralled her? Giving her a chance to break free and get help didn't make any sense. It gave others the opportunity to notice something was wrong. Why risk it? The answer hit me, and my breath flew from my chest like I'd been struck with a sudden weight.

It was part of his game.

The risk, the thrill of making her come back to him, the possession of another's will. That's why he did it. Sick bastard. As I pulled into Sylvester's parking lot, I gripped the steering wheel tighter. The freak was going to pay.

• • •

Only one car sat in Sylvester's parking lot—not surprising, since it was just nearing lunchtime, and they weren't known for their food. The club probably wouldn't be in full swing and fully staffed until ten o'clock. I debated coming back later when we'd have a better chance of catching people with information, but I didn't have the patience. I slammed the car door, and then walked up to Aidan.

He stepped out of the Jeep and shut the door behind him. His hair was tousled from the constant Chicago breeze, and I wondered if that's how he looked when he rolled out of bed in the morning. Five o'clock shadow added to the image, and I had the sudden urge to run my hand through his hair to smooth it.

I took a deep breath and forced my thoughts back to the case. What the hell was I doing? Every time I looked at the man I struggled not to touch him. I was a damn nymphomaniac lately.

I tromped up to the bar door and knocked—banging the side of my fist against the rough wood.

A tall, wide man answered the knock. He looked like he could probably toss a patron out of the bar with very little effort. He carried some extra weight around his middle, but appeared solid rather than obese. Sweat beaded on his bald head, forming droplets that ran down the side of his face. He held a broom in one hand and propped the door open with the other to look at me.

"We're not open 'til one," he said, gesturing toward the faded metal sign hanging next to the door.

I pulled my badge out and flashed it at him. "We need to ask you a few questions."

He frowned then stepped back so we could enter.

"I'm Jay Lawson, and I manage the club. What's this about?" he asked, as we walked into the small area that served as a restaurant until the bar really got going. The decor looked like it was updated in the late 70s, and the dark hardwood floors and old cash register sitting on the corner of the counter made me think townie bar—not happening club.

I pulled Amanda's picture from my pocket. "Have you seen this woman? She would have been in here Monday night…probably not alone."

He glanced at the picture. "I wasn't in Monday; you'll have to talk to my daughter."

"Is she here?"

"Not 'til three or so."

"We're going to need you to call her and ask her to come in early," Aidan said from behind me.

The bar owner snorted. "That girl don't come in early for no reason."

I took a step toward him and looked at his face, giving

him my best cop stare: hard eyes and a no-nonsense line set on my mouth. "She'll make an exception today." Or I would go knock on her door and haul her here.

"Fine," he said. "Don't mind dragging her out of bed early anyhow."

Aidan turned to me as the bar owner went to call the girl. "I'm going to go, check with my sources. Call me if you need anything. Otherwise I'll track you down later."

"Fine by me."

He gripped my shoulders and I started. He leaned in and I stopped breathing. But he bypassed my mouth, his rough cheek touching mine as he moved. Lips a hairbreadth from my ear, he whispered, "You will call me, right? If you get a lead, don't go after this guy alone."

I nodded, unable to think of a suitable reply. After one final squeeze of my arms, he left.

Nearly an hour ticked by before the manager's daughter showed up. A long hour where I was left with nothing to do but remember the pressure of Aidan's hands on my arms, and the roughness of his cheeks sliding against mine. By then I was ready to strangle the girl, but willing to overlook her attitude if she had information for me. She was shorter than me, which was an accomplishment all its own. A pretty thing, she had blond hair that dangled nearly to her waist with bangs that hung into her eyes. I couldn't begin to describe the ways such a haircut would annoy me.

"Ms. Lawson?"

"I'm Kimmy," she said. Her pert nose stuck up in the air, like she thought she was doing me a favor by deigning to talk to me.

I handed her the picture of Amanda. "Do you remember

seeing her here on Monday night?"

She stared at the picture for a few seconds, and her eyes widened. "Oh yes, I remember her. She was here with the hottie." She smirked. "Guy was quite a catch, but he sure had straying on his mind, if you know what I mean."

I mentally congratulated my gut. The killer was a man— so almost definitely an incubus. "Explain it to me."

"Well she was all over him, hanging on his every word, you know? But every time she'd go to the bathroom, he was all over me. Talking to me, flirting with me, looking at me with those eyes." Kimmy sighed, a smile turning up the corners of her mouth.

"Can you describe him?"

"Oh, he was hot. Dark hair, dark blue eyes. The bluest eyes you've ever seen," she said, with a dreamy look.

"How tall?"

"He was pretty tall, maybe six feet."

My stomach tensed and my thoughts turned to Aidan. Dark blue eyes, tall? But, no. He was OWEA.

But he wouldn't be the first cop in history to turn bad.

"Scars or tattoos? Any other features you can remember?" I said, keeping my voice as even as I could manage.

"No scars or tats that I could see…though I wouldn't have minded a closer look, if you know what I mean." She grinned. "Normally, I don't dig long hair on a guy, but he pulled it off."

"His hair was long?"

"Maybe as long as mine, pulled back in a ponytail against his neck."

I remembered to breathe. That didn't match Aidan. His hair was long around his face, but nothing like the hair she'd described on Amanda's date. He might have worn a wig, but he didn't strike me as the kind of guy who'd be caught dead in one. The eyes matched, but he wasn't the only guy in the world with nice eyes.

"Have you ever seen him in here before?" I kept my voice steady. Goody for me.

"Oh yeah, one other time. He had a different date then, not as flashy as the one on Monday. A player, that guy is, but I'd play with him any day of the week." The dreamy expression was back. The incubus was good, I'd give him that.

Kimmy followed me to my Toyota, where I showed her a picture of the first victim.

"Could be her, I guess." She shrugged. "Honestly she was such a wallflower I don't remember."

I quizzed Kimmy for the better part of the next hour, and then let her get to work with instructions to call me immediately if the man showed his face in the bar again. She promised to call, but only after I told her that the women in the pictures were dead, and the handsome stranger may have killed them.

• • •

I drove to Amanda's house next, telling myself I should take a quick look around the scene to make sure the investigators hadn't missed anything. I parked a street over from hers and walked to the house, sneaking into the backyard. Feeling a bit of déjà vu, I slid my driver's license between her doorknob and frame and let myself in.

Her kitchen was in a worse state than she'd left it. The police had dusted for prints and searched for evidence, leaving a mess of fingerprint powder and rifled cupboards in their wake. Amanda would be pissed to see her home this way.

Keeping my breathing steady, I walked through her house and tried to picture what had happened to her. We'd found the incubus's second victim on Sunday night, and Amanda was killed Monday night. The murderer liked to play with his victims for a period of time before actually killing them, but Amanda didn't act like she was under anyone's influence but her own only a night before her death. And she'd sounded tired in the voice mail she left me, not thralled.

I frowned and walked into her bedroom. The comforter was still indented where her body had waited to be discovered for over twelve hours after her death. Touching the comforter where her neck had lain, her head hanging over to stare at the bedroom door, I wished there was someone else I could talk to about the case. But I had no friends to speak of, outside of Amanda and my other coworkers, and my father and stepmother didn't like to hear anything about my work. They had made that abundantly clear over the years.

I replayed in my mind the last time I'd seen Amanda, searching for a clue that would suggest she was already under the incubus's influence. But she didn't have any of the signs. No dreamy expression, no distracted mannerisms, no talk of a beautiful man and his dark blue eyes. She handled the crime scene with her normal efficiency and solidity, even thinking quickly enough to snag the bit of hair from the victim to run a spell tracer on. Could I have missed a subtle hint?

The spell tracer. I pulled Amanda's file from my bag and glanced through the evidence list. No mention of a bit of hair that didn't belong to Amanda. No evidence baggy. That would have certainly been recorded. Her spell kit was listed, and there was nothing obvious missing from it. Suddenly, I wished I had a better understanding of witchcraft.

Was the hair already gone because she'd used it? Had she traced the bastard down to his den?

"Did you confront him without me?" I whispered.

I hissed. It fit. That's why he'd selected a cop—an otherworlder with the ability to defend herself both with her witchcraft and the power of the law. Not to mention her sidearm. She didn't fit his victim profile, or his modus operandi. He killed her because he had to. Because she found his ass and was going to bring him in.

It was fast, too. I went through the timeline in my head. Sunday night, we met at the second victim's house, where Amanda took the sample of her hair. Monday morning, I'd gone to the Medical Examiner's and talked to Marisol, while Amanda prepped her tracking spell. Monday at lunchtime, Amanda stood me up for lunch—she was on his trail by then. Monday afternoon, I interviewed the second victim's boyfriend, Jason, while Amanda ate a late lunch. Sometime between my lunch at The Grill House and Amanda's, she'd caught up to the incubus and he'd enthralled her. Monday evening, Amanda met back up with the incubus at Sylvester's. She took him home, made dinner for him.

The image of the two plates floated back into my mind. One practically licked clean, the other only partially finished. Amanda was usually a good eater—the late lunch, of course. She'd made the meal for him. She wasn't hungry. Then he'd taken her in her room. Drained her dry while she probably begged him for more.

My stomach heaved, and I ran for the bathroom, barely making it to the toilet before I vomited. I rinsed out my mouth in her sink and dried my eyes. The bastard was going to pay for reducing her to something that couldn't think for herself. For using her like a battery to recharge himself. For taking away my friend.

I grabbed her hairbrush from the bathroom drawer and walked back to the kitchen. I wasn't technically stealing evidence from a crime scene. Not an active one, anyway. The police had been here and left, and I needed something that was closely connected to Amanda. I was no expert on spell ingredients, but objects didn't get much more personal than DNA. I shoved the file back into my bag and tucked the brush into a side pocket. Giving the room a last glance, I headed for the door.

. . .

After some cursing, a bit of luck, and a few trips around the block, I found a parking spot in front of the downtown high-rise where Natalie Leigh's office was located. The property reeked of money, and the lobby had that new building smell to it—fresh paint and new carpet. The building looked newer than some, but not *that* new. I gave the receptionist a quick nod, but couldn't force a polite smile onto my face. "Natalie Leigh's office?"

"Identification, please." Her voice was nasally, and her nose was red. Despite her obvious cold, she kept her fake, perky smile in place.

I grimaced and pulled my badge out and flashed it at her. One advantage of being an otherworlder was immunity to most human diseases. But it didn't make being around normals with a runny nose any less disgusting.

She gestured toward the elevators. "Fourteenth floor. As you exit the elevator, turn right. Her office is all the way at the end of the hall."

"Thanks," I muttered, and headed for the elevator. The receptionist picked up her phone, no doubt to warn Natalie of my impending arrival.

My cell started ringing while I waited for the elevator to arrive. I flipped it open and put it to my ear. "Confirmed with the bar owner's daughter that we're looking for a man. That'll teach you to doubt my gut," I said without preamble.

Aidan whistled. "Nice info to have. Get anything else?"

"I'm working on something now. You got any info for me?"

"Not much. Just that we can't find anyone staying at hotels near Sylvester's that matches what we're looking for. No one who's been there for several weeks. No one acting suspiciously."

The elevator dinged. "Look, let's talk later. I gotta go."

The fourteenth floor was as nicely decorated as the first, with matching sconces on the walls and the same dark and light green carpets swirled together to form geometric designs. But this floor lacked the scent of new paint. Instead, it smelled of upholstery and carpet and computers—like most offices.

As the receptionist said, the etched glass door at the end of the hallway had Natalie Leigh's name inscribed on it, with one word below her name to denote her occupation.

Witch.

I opened the door and slipped through. I expected to see another receptionist, but there was only a waiting room equipped with padded chairs and small stands holding old *People* and *Time* magazines.

The door at the other end of the room stood open, and as I took a step toward it, a voice called out.

"Come in, Detective."

The woman behind the cherry desk didn't look like a formidable witch. She especially didn't look worth the undoubtedly astounding rate she charged the police department for her services.

Witches—real witches—weren't cheap.

Not that Amanda hadn't been a real witch. She could hold her own. But amateur witches like Amanda were self-taught. Covenant witches were trained since birth, pledged to their particular branch of magic, and raised from bloodlines that could be traced back into prehistory. They were as inhuman as I was—or more.

The witch's short, dark hair gave her a tomboyish appearance, but her face was pretty and heart-shaped, delicate. No one would mistake her for a man, even if her frame hadn't been so slight. Her light green eyes stood out in stark contrast to her dark hair and golden skin, making her gaze almost startling. She stood behind the desk and held out her hand to me. As we shook, I took in the rest of her. She stood even shorter than me—maybe five feet tall—and she wore an expensive-looking green blouse and black slacks. The blouse, I noticed, matched her eyes. Not to mention the carpet.

"I'm Natalie Leigh. Please call me Natalie. Detective,

how can I help the police department today?" Her voice was soft and lilting. I would have bet the witch could sing.

"I'm Detective Kiera McLoughlin. I need your help finding a killer."

She narrowed her eyes. Cute or no, the witch was no fool. "I haven't received any paperwork. No notification you were coming." She grinned, and the expression was almost feral. "No check."

I gritted my teeth and concentrated on not pulling my gun. "Well, you wouldn't have. I'm hiring you myself, outside of the department." I hesitated, but something told me that she would know if I lied. "My partner was recently killed, and I've been taken off the case. The PD won't hire you except as a last resort, because you're too damn expensive. Her killer may be gone by then."

Natalie leaned back in her chair and watched me. I stifled the urge to tap my foot or play with my fingernails, or something equally annoying, and watched her right back.

"As you said, Detective, I'm damn expensive. And locator spells are particularly pricey." She waved a hand in the air. "Rare ingredients, you understand. You are prepared to pay my fee?"

"Yes," I said through my clenched jaw.

"Fine, I think you're good for it. Did you bring something of the victim's? Or even better, an item belonging to the killer?"

I snorted. "Yeah, like I'd be coming to your expensive ass if I had something of his."

Natalie laughed, a musical sound, and only the knowledge of how much she was going to deplete my savings account dispelled her charm. Locator spells were much easier if you had an item owned by the person you searched for. Any amateur witch would have been able to pull that off. Trying to find them with something that was only second-arily connected to the target of the spell — like an item from someone they killed — required talent.

And my brave partner had tried it without a second thought.

The hairbrush was still in the side pocket I'd pushed it into. The pocket was one I didn't use much so there was little chance of the space having anything of mine inside to mess up the energy or whatever witches used that would connect the hair in the brush with its owner. I set it gingerly on the desk and watched Natalie expectantly.

"How long since she used this?"

"Couldn't be more than a couple of days."

"Good. Follow me and bring it with you, please."

Natalie led the way through the door in the side of her office that I'd mistaken for a bathroom when I'd first walked in. It led to a short hallway, with a bathroom on one side and a closed door on the other. By the size of the door I guessed it led to a closet. At the end of the hall was another room, this one even bigger than her office. Shelves lined the room, covering more than half of the walls. Where the shelves were absent, complicated glyphs could be seen, each intricately drawn.

Her casting room.

The circle appeared to be etched into the floor rather than just painted on. Some of the glyphs brushed on the walls were white, the others red. I grimaced at the red ones. In the poor lighting they looked like they'd been drawn in blood.

"It's not blood," Natalie said, voice full of amusement. "It's not regular paint either, but I promise it's all plant based."

She hummed while she pulled ingredients off the shelves and started painting a symbol in the center of the circle. Her soft voice barely carried to me, and I wondered if she even knew she hummed.

"Okay then." She stepped back from the symbol she'd been drawing and turned to me. "I need you to tell me everything you know about the person we're looking for. Is he human? Otherworlder?"

"Otherworlder."

"What kind?"

I hesitated. Telling her he was probably an incubus might get me booted from her office. At the very least she wasn't likely to take me seriously. "We don't know for sure. Something that can kill without leaving marks." That at least, was the truth.

"So not a vampire then? Could he be a witch?"

I just stared at her for a moment. I hadn't even considered the possibility that the killer was a witch. I was pretty sure that only a Covenant witch would be capable of killing someone with magic, especially by draining their psychic energy. And Covenant witches were rare—not as rare as a species that by most accounts was extinct—but still rare. And ones with the power to kill without leaving a trace? They must be rarer still. A brief image of Natalie standing over Amanda's prone body flashed in my mind. No. The witch could have done it—maybe. But she struck me as too smart to kill in her own backyard. "Not a vamp for sure," I said. "What are the odds that a witch powerful enough to kill several women without making a mark got under whatever radar you guys have on the city?"

She gave me a thin smile. "Not likely. A witch powerful enough to kill like that and evade detection? I can count the ones living in this country on one hand. And none of them are likely suspects."

"An amateur witch couldn't have—"

She held up a hand and looked like she was trying not to laugh from the sheer insanity of my suggestion. "Not possible."

"Good. Then I'd say we're not looking for a witch, either."

She replaced some of the bottles she'd removed from the shelf and took down a metal plate that had little feet on the underside to prop it up, and then waved me into the circle.

"Before we begin, I want to remind you there is only a very small chance this will work. And I cannot assume responsibility for any unforeseen consequences that may arise from the spell."

I nodded. "Yeah, got it."

She frowned. "I know you must miss your partner. But this is a tricky spell in the best of times. And I require payment regardless of outcome."

"Just cast the damn spell."

The witch nodded and grabbed Amanda's brush from the floor and set it next to where she knelt. She pulled a city map from a small stack on the shelf and unfolded it, and then set the paper on the floor to her left. She placed the small metal plate in the middle of the circle, on top of the symbol, and dumped a pile of herbs and small pieces of wood onto of the rough surface.

Natalie whispered a word and lit a wooden match.

"Kneel," she ordered.

As I knelt across from her, she tossed the match onto the plate.

The pile of tinder exploded into a small fire, filling the air with the scent of lemons and sage, which combined with the other scents and made the air rushing into my lungs smell almost medicinal. I let out a small cough to clear the taste from my throat, but it didn't help.

Natalie closed her eyes and murmured something I couldn't make out. She pulled a handful of Amanda's hair from the brush and tossed it onto the fire. A few more strands went onto the map.

Holding her palms up in front of her, she waved her fingers at me until I gripped her hands in mine.

"Close your eyes."

I closed them and tried to steady my breathing. The overpowering herbs grew stronger, burning their way down my throat and into my lungs.

"Concentrate. Visualize your partner, what she meant to you, how much you miss her."

Amanda's face filled my mind's eye, as if summoned by the witch: her sardonic grin and steady personality, her long hair and devotion to her job. Her wide, unblinking eyes. Her tangled hair hanging over the edge of her bed.

I swallowed around the lump in my throat.

"Yes," Natalie said softly. "Now I will guide your intent. Concentrate on him. The killer who took her from you. Feel how much you need to find him."

I forced myself to see her, to picture Amanda. And I thought of him, the man who killed her. How badly I wanted to return the favor. I felt it all. The pain and rage and fear.

It was as if Natalie had opened a floodgate, and maybe she had, perhaps that was part of the spell. I didn't know. I concentrated, blinking back tears that came more from emotion than the heavy burning of herbs in the air, and through it all Natalie hummed.

The hair on my body pricked up, and I felt goose bumps rise to cover my arms. I heard a buzzing sound, and struggled to keep my focus. The space around us vibrated, and I could no longer smell the herbs. Instead, everything reeked of burnt things. The spell hit me with a blast of energy that skittered its way up my arms and into my body. The air pushed from my lungs as if a great weight pressed against me. I couldn't breathe, but I didn't care because the energy felt *so good*. Painful yet powerful, as if before that moment I'd never felt anything real, only shadows of what living was supposed to feel like. I struggled to keep my focus on Amanda, on her killer. Then, as if someone clicked a light switch, the weight was gone. Nothing crawled up my arms begging to be freed, no energy pulsed through me.

I gasped and blinked stupidly at the witch, my brain fuzzy from the force of her spell. "Jeez," I managed after a few moments. "Could've warned me."

But the witch wasn't paying attention to me; she was frowning at the map. "Just as I thought," she murmured.

"What?" She didn't answer me, so I reached out and grabbed the map and scanned it. The surface was perfect. No marks scarred it. Nothing showed it hadn't come new off the shelf only minutes before.

"I take it something was supposed to happen to this?" I stared at the map. Then I tossed it back down and struggled to my feet. "What happened? I thought you were a powerful witch?"

She shook her head, and then pushed herself up and dusted off her knees. "It didn't work. Whoever you're looking for is powerful. Powerful and possessing no small amount of psychic energy."

"Now you're telling me he's psychic?"

She looked at me like I'd said something especially stupid and took a deep breath. "No. I'm saying he's full of energy and he knows how to use it to protect himself. Lots of things can accumulate energy, though few to that degree. Are you sure he isn't a vampire?"

"He's not a freaking vampire. I told you that!" I took a breath and lowered my voice. "I think he might be an incubus."

She raised an eyebrow. "An incubus who has drained how many women to the point of death?"

"Maybe a dozen."

"Well that would have been good information to have, Detective."

I threw my hands up. "What difference would it have made? Other than making you think I was nuts?"

"I would no sooner try an open trace spell on an incubus full of psychic energy than I would on a vampire who had been draining victims at that rate. It's dangerous. It's possible for a creature like that, with appropriate knowledge and training, to use such a spell against you. And almost impossible for you to actually succeed in using it against him—not without something of his to use as a focus."

"My partner found him and she was a freaking amateur!" My voice rose to a yell, but I couldn't help it. How the hell was I supposed to find him now?

Natalie raised an eyebrow and crossed her arms. "Did she really? I don't think so, Detective. I suspect she tried, probably using the hair of a victim like we did here. But she wasn't a Covenant witch, and not equipped with the same defenses I created for us. She opened a doorway and found something stronger than her. She didn't find and track him with that spell. He used that spell to track *her*."

My mouth dropped open, and I stared at the witch.

She sighed. "I'm sorry. I'm sure your friend was a good amateur witch. But few outside of the Covenant realize such a thing is possible."

"And you don't think he'll find me the same way?"

"Not with the precautions I took. And as the caster he would only be able to trace it to me, not to you." She sounded convincing, but a bit of doubt nagged at me, adding to my frustration.

I wanted to scream, use the power of my voice to destroy her baubles and bottles and the precious spell ingredients within them, but such a display would have been childish, and wrong. Amanda's death wasn't her fault. And screaming would only further hurt my bank account.

So I kept my mouth shut, shook the witch's hand, and left.

Chapter Seven

After leaving Natalie's, I drove around for a while, trying to focus my thoughts. Giving up on that, I stopped at Sylvester's to make sure the incubus hadn't been there. Kimmy looked at me like I was a nut, considering it was only six o'clock. I ordered a sandwich to go and headed home.

By the time I got there, I felt like I'd run a marathon. Spell casting required energy and since I had the strongest intent—an important thing in witchcraft—Natalie had used mine for the spell, intermingled with her own to direct the magic. I considered what fueled her side of the energy, and decided that anyone would have a good amount of motivation with the exorbitant fee she charged. I wondered if she'd have had the same intent on an hourly wage.

My keys clanked when I tossed them on the coffee table. Cold beer in hand, I sat down to consider my next move. I could go to the bar, in the hope that he'd show with a new date or come in seeking one, but that was a long shot. After taking a cop there the night she died, he would almost definitely avoid the place like the plague now. In fact, he'd probably head out of town, if he were at all smart.

The doorbell sounded, interrupting my thoughts. I checked the peephole, and then sighed and turned the deadbolt. I opened the door a crack to peer out at the man on my front step.

"What?"

"Wow, so welcoming. I'm amazed you don't have men beating down your door with that attitude."

I gritted my teeth and stepped away from the door. I walked back to the couch and plopped down. Aidan could come in or go straight to hell for all I cared at that moment. I took a long drink from my beer, nearly finishing it, and I heard the door click shut.

"You all right?" He sat down on the couch next to me, not touching, but oh, so close.

"I'm fine." I shook my head to clear the cobwebs. What was wrong with me? My friend is dead for two days and I was ready to jump someone I barely knew?

"You don't look fine."

"Yeah, well, it's been a shitty week."

He got up from the couch and disappeared into the kitchen. When he reappeared, he carried two bottles of beer. Handing me one, he took a sip from the other.

I teetered between feeling annoyed at him for acting so comfortable in my house and happy he got me a fresh beer. The lure of the cold liquid proved too good to stay irritated, so I settled for a quiet seething while I nursed it.

"Want to talk about it?"

"Not particularly." I pressed the bottle against my head

and wished I could have a redo of the last few days. "Like I told you on the phone, I got the incubus's description from Kimmy. He took the first local victim—Claire Simons—to Sylvester's, too. Not sure about the second one."

Aidan didn't say anything; he just watched me with his dark eyes and sipped his beer. God, he was attractive. My heart raced just looking at him—even while talking about my murdered friend and partner. Ridiculous.

It's stress, I told myself. Stress plays havoc with emotions and hormones.

"He likes to toy with his victims. The first two were acting odd for several days before they were killed. He thralls them, then hunts them."

"You think the fact they could escape gives him a thrill?"

"Yes."

"But you said your partner seemed fine the night before she died. She didn't act like she was under any kind of influence." He took a longer drink from his beer, and then swallowed and stared at me, gaze running down from my face to my body.

Ignoring the tingling along my spine his eyes elicited, I said, "No, she didn't. I think she wasn't a victim he planned on. I think he killed her out of necessity. He didn't play with her as long."

"Necessity?"

"Yes. Amanda didn't match his other victims. She was a cop and a witch. Tough as nails. She did bodybuilding for a hobby. She was a black belt. Nothing about her suggested she was a normal, weak human." I stifled a gasp as he reached out and pushed a chunk of my hair behind my ear, scooting closer to me.

"Why her? He hasn't gone after investigators before," he said in a low voice. "Except our psychic, and she wasn't exactly a badass cop."

"She took some of the last victim's hair with her when she left the scene, and was going to try a locator spell using it. Whatever she did, it must have led her to him." *Or him to her*, I mentally amended, remembering Natalie's warning.

He frowned. "Makes sense. But then why did he send her out at all? She went to the restaurant by herself. Maybe other places."

"I think he still needed to get some kind of thrill out of it. He's driven to kill a certain way. Maybe he wanted the rush. Needed it. Especially because of who she was, and how powerful she was. Might give him an even better high than the weaker victims." I considered telling Aidan about the spell I'd cast with Natalie, but it seemed pointless. It hadn't worked, after all.

"Perhaps." He leaned in closer to me. "Which means he might be even more dangerous now, and expand his list of potential victims."

"Might…make him slip up," I said, trying to keep my voice steady.

"We can hope." He took the empty beer bottle from my hand and set it on the coffee table along with his. I almost sighed when he moved away from me. Out of relief or disappointment, I wasn't sure.

My relief, if that's what it was, proved short-lived. He leaned back toward me and lowered his face to mine.

I took in a quick, short breath and looked up into his eyes. They were dark pools that would drown me if I let them, but I couldn't pull myself away. Scratch that, I didn't want to pull myself away. I wanted him to kiss me.

"You're irresistible," he whispered, his voice caressing me. "I promised myself I'd leave you alone, but I cannot." He lowered his lips to mine. It was a soft kiss, but it lit a match inside of me.

I deepened the kiss, opening my mouth to his. His tongue slipped between my lips and stroked mine. A moan escaped me, and my arms found their way around his neck. He tensed even as I relaxed in his arms.

He pulled back from me and stared at my face. His lips were slightly parted and his eyes were heavily lidded. His breathing came in harsh gasps. He looked passionate, seductive, and in painful need. Did I look the same to him?

"If you want me to leave, tell me now," he whispered, stroking my hair with his hand.

I answered without thinking, but it was an honest reply. "I want you to stay."

He smiled, a fierce expression that was wholly male. "Good."

His mouth took mine forcefully, all hesitation gone, and I returned his force, pushing all of the emotions that assailed me into the kiss. He tasted of peppermint and alcohol, and it intermingled with the scent of him to overwhelm me.

Warm hands pushed me into the couch. The cushions were soft against my back, contrasting against the hardness of his body on my front. As he licked and nibbled his way down my neck, pausing to suck softly on my collarbone, my skin tingled. He moved back and I cried out in protest, but he silenced me with a grin and a kiss before tugging my shirt over my head.

"Here?" I gasped, giving the living room a quick glance

as he cupped my breast, running his finger over the lace at the top of my bra.

"Here," he growled in agreement, and he grasped my knees, pulling me closer to the edge of the couch. Then he slipped between my legs and took my breast in his mouth.

I couldn't think, couldn't do anything but feel him sucking and biting at my nipple through the thin fabric. Hot and wet, I could scarcely believe how my body reacted to him. Since he'd shown up I'd had only a tenuous hold on my self-control. When was the last time I'd felt like this?

I hadn't, I realized, and the thought hit me like a splash of cold water.

Aidan raised his eyes, as if sensing the change in me. He took one look at my face and shook his head. "No thinking," he said, tipping my chin, and then he took my mouth with his again.

He kissed me until I forgot my fear, his hands straying to stroke my sides, and then back to my breasts. The lacy bra unlatched in the front, and he made short work of it. As he pulled back to take my bare chest in with his eyes, I reached for his shirt, tugging it free of his pants.

He revealed muscular shoulders and a smooth chest when he pulled the shirt over his head. Somehow he looked bigger without the T-shirt hiding him, and suddenly I felt very small.

When he helped me to my feet, he seemed to tower over me. Then he knelt in front of me and pulled my pants down over my hips, bringing my thong with them. When I was free of my clothing, he settled back on his heels and raked his eyes over my body. I couldn't feel embarrassed, not with those hungry eyes all over me, wanting me.

"You're so beautiful," he whispered, and then he pushed up to his feet and wrapped his arms around me. His body was hard against mine, the soft skin of his chest held me, but his jeans were rough. I ached for that roughness, and couldn't help rubbing my body against his erection.

He cursed and yanked off his jeans. Then he stopped for a moment, only a couple of feet in front of me. As he watched me take in his body, a smile touched his lips. A smug look of a man who knew he was being admired.

Heat touched my cheeks and I tore my gaze from him and looked at the floor. He chuckled, and moved to me. Fingertips touched under my chin, and I raised my eyes to meet his. I glared at him, and his smile widened.

"You never have to be embarrassed with me."

I raised an eyebrow, and he pulled me back into his arms so fast I squeaked. His tongue met mine and then I felt his arm under my knees. In one quick motion, he picked me up then laid me on the carpet.

My objections were forgotten when he turned his attention to my breasts again, plucking and pinching and sucking them until they were taut and red. The gentleness had disappeared, and there was no amusement in his expression. I reached for him, wrapping my hand around his erection, squeezing the base before running my fingertips lightly to the moist tip.

I wanted—needed—to forget all the bad. Just for a while.

His hand moved to palm between my legs and I cried out at the small touch. When was the last time I'd felt this enflamed, this out of control? Had I ever?

Moving from my grip, he lowered his head and nipped at me. He licked my most sensitive spot with quick, confident touches of his tongue. But the touch was too light, and I was close — so close — to release.

"Please," I gasped.

"Please what?" he whispered, looking up at me from between my knees. The expression on his face was almost bestial, like he wanted nothing more than to shove me down and drive into me until I begged him to stop. Just the thought almost pushed me over the edge.

"Fuck me," I demanded, desperation making my voice hoarse.

He growled and then he was on top of me, pushing my legs farther apart with his hips, taking my mouth with his. I'd never been more grateful in my life for OWs' immunity to human disease — or for my consistent use of birth control despite my lack of a sex life.

I turned my face from him, gasping for breath as he pushed his cock into me, gentle for a few, agonizing seconds, and then as his fingers dug into the carpet, he thrust himself into my tightness, forcing my body to take him fully.

"Aidan!" I cried, and he moved his hands to grip my shoulders, holding me in place as I raised my hips to meet him. His chest rubbed against my sensitive breasts, pushing me to the brink. And when he slipped a hand between us to touch me, I exploded. He stiffened above me, and then drove himself into me, his body spasming.

Chapter Eight

I wasn't entirely sure what pissed me off more that morning, the fact I'd experienced maybe the best sex of my life only to wake up to an empty pillow, or that I was dragged out of my comfortable bed by a phone call from my irate boss at six o'clock in the morning. It was a toss-up, really.

Waiting outside Lieutenant Vasquez's office for a half hour after I hauled myself to the precinct certainly didn't help things, especially considering how little rest I'd gotten the night before. I rubbed the sleep from my eyes and stared at my coffee cup while I waited.

Last night had been amazing—even trying to tell myself that it was only because I was highly emotional from losing a close friend didn't quite meet the sniff test. Aidan was just as good in bed as his dark eyes suggested he would be, and then some. Worse, I felt safe during the time he held me. We talked for hours, and while some of the details were a bit fuzzy, I confided more in him than I had in anyone for a long time. Then, this morning when the phone rang, he was gone. The other side of the bed was cold, only the wrinkled pillow suggesting he had been there at all.

I was an idiot.

You're an adult; you can sleep with whomever you want, I told myself. That was true—I was no prude—but the talking…it made me too close to a man I still didn't know enough about.

The door to the lieutenant's office swung open, startling me from my thoughts. A uniform stepped out and gave me a small wave as he passed. I couldn't remember his name offhand, but I'd seen him around. Giving him a quick nod, I got up and headed into Vasquez's office.

"Sit down, Mac."

I sat. "Good morning to you too, Lieutenant." Seemed I wasn't the only one in a mood today.

He shot me a warning glance, but ignored my rib. "I'm going to do you a favor, and in return you're going to do one for me."

I leaned back and took a sip of my coffee. Whatever he wanted must be urgent for him to be at the office before seven o'clock.

"I'm going to pretend you weren't seen leaving Amanda Franklin's house yesterday afternoon." I opened my mouth to speak and he raised a hand. "And you're going to go out and do your damn job today. I've got a tag and bag for you. We're low on resources with a cop killer on the loose. And you obviously need to be kept busy or you'll get yourself into trouble."

I gritted my teeth. A tag and bag was a collar I'd normally jump for the chance at—something Lieutenant Vasquez knew quite well—but I didn't need the distraction from Amanda's investigation right now.

"Should be quick," he continued. "We've got a problem down in Willowbrook. You know it?"

I nodded. Willowbrook was south of the station, an older neighborhood full of middle class families.

"Pets have been disappearing; people's garbage has been tossed. You get the picture."

"Sounds like a kobold, hobgoblin, or some other pest. I don't think a detective is—"

"I didn't ask for your thoughts, Detective. I'm giving you a job to keep you out of my hair. Did you really think we didn't have your partner's house watched?"

I didn't know what to say, so I kept my mouth shut.

"Look. This isn't glamorous work. It's probably just a pest, like you said. But someone needs to take care of it, and I need to keep you busy. Deal with it." He tossed a file in my general direction and nodded to the door. "Talk to the people in the neighborhood. Call for backup if you get anything solid to follow up on."

The temptation to argue with him almost overwhelmed me, but I'd get back to Amanda's case faster by finishing the tag and bag than I would arguing with the Lieutenant. With any luck, it would be a hobgoblin or a brownie, an easy fix with the right gear, and I'd be back on the incubus by the afternoon.

• • •

It took longer than I had hoped to find out exactly what I hunted and where it might be hiding. After interviewing several families on the street, and one unfortunate trek through a nearby wooded area complete with a crawl through a tight storm drain, I was ready to finish this hunt.

The house was dark, the small bit of light from the streetlamps blocked by the blinds, and the second the door opened the stench hit me. Rotting meat, old garbage, waste, and a metallic overtone meant blood. It smelled like a text-book revenant den — but I wasn't hunting a revenant. No one had died in this neighborhood in months, according to the neighbors, and none in this house. Revenants were always drawn back to their own homes or a place dear to them. Staring into the dark, I ignored the odor and pushed the door so it stood wide open. The light from the street lamps did little to illuminate the stinking hole, so I pulled a small flashlight from my belt. I reached up and yanked my gun from my shoulder holster with my other hand and stepped into the den.

I considered waiting for the backup I'd called only a minute ago, but decided against it. Backup would almost certainly be slow. The critter could escape by the time they got here. Besides, the day I couldn't take out a hobgoblin or kobold on my own was the day I would give up my badge and retire.

A hobgoblin likely hid in the foreclosed and abandoned home I walked into. A disappearing pet or two might not be beyond the realm of a kobold or a brownie — they would hunt if starved — but this thing seemed to prefer pets to garbage. That was unlikely for the scavenging creatures, who strongly preferred to pick through human garbage over having to kill something. This neighborhood was full of trash, set out in front of dozens of homes weekly for the garbage men. A hobgoblin was the only thing that made sense.

I trudged past the front door into the living room. The source of the smells wasn't here. The area was relatively clean-looking, marred only by the odor hanging in the air. Moving quietly through the house, I checked the rooms one by one. The kitchen was the only place that showed any use. It was a mess, but not the creature's primary feeding ground. It looked like its food—both trash and animal—had been dragged over the light tile. The trail led from the back door to another door in the kitchen. I grimaced. It almost certainly led to the basement. Hobgoblins and their ilk always gravitated toward dark places, strongly preferring underground areas.

I gripped the doorknob, cringing as I felt a sticky substance under my fingers, and opened the door. The smell hit me—so much worse than the rest of the house. I swallowed and breathed slowly. Vomiting here would be something I wouldn't live down for a long time. My small flashlight revealed stairs that disappeared into the darkness. I sensed something down there, looking up at me. Ignoring the creepy chills it sent down my spine, I held my gun out in front of me and started down.

"Police," I called, figuring I might as well announce myself, since the hobgoblin already knew I was here. The small-brained little bastard would probably ignore my authority as an officer of the law, but it never hurt to give it a shot.

I gagged as I entered the basement. Animal carcasses in various states of decay littered the floor. Shredded trash bags and their contents were spread around as well. Not a square inch of space on the floor remained uncovered by filth. Walking down there would mean wading through trash up to my ankles throughout, and up to my knees in many places. Standing on the last step, brilliant ideas that would not require me to walk in the filth flashed through my head. Could I burn it out? Scream it out? Just go back upstairs and wait for the little bugger to come to me?

The scavenger took the choice from me. Something hard slammed into me from my side, knocking me into the basement. My gun flew from my hand, landing somewhere in the mess of trash and animal parts. I cursed and tried to pry the thing off me, still gripping the flashlight in one hand.

The creature was big. It didn't make any sense. Hobgoblins were only two to three feet tall and they were solid, but never anywhere near this heavy. I got a leg between us and pushed, tossing the creature off, behind me and to the side. I was suddenly very thankful that Amanda insisted I go to karate classes with her.

Gripping the flashlight I turned it to the area where I'd thrown the creature. Nothing. Damn, it was fast. I cursed under my breath and searched the floor for my gun, crouching to minimize how big of a target I presented.

As something moved past me, air licked my side. I turned just in time to see a large shape take off up the stairs.

So much for the hobgoblin theory.

Taking the stairs two at a time, I pursued the creature, tripping on the last step. I picked myself up, knees protesting, and headed for the wide-open back door. As I ran I cursed myself for not subduing it when it was confined— using my scream if necessary. It would be much more difficult and dangerous to scream in the open. I whipped out the back door, but got only a few feet before a weight hit me from behind, throwing me to the ground. Wind knocked out of me, I struggled to pull in enough breath to scream. The creature bit at my neck, its breath rancid.

It was gone as suddenly as it appeared, and a crash sounded behind me. I struggled to my knees, and turned to look around. The streetlights and moon gave the backyard of the abandoned building an eerie glow, but it was an improvement over the pitch-black darkness of the basement. My attacker lay in a heap against the side of the house, and a figure—my rescuer—stood between the creature and me. His dark hair moved in the wind. He'd set his body in a defensive stance—legs widely set with his side facing the monster lying on the ground.

Aidan.

"Are you okay?" he asked.

Annoyance flashed through me. Who did he think he was? He left me without so much as a by your leave after a night filled with fantastic sex, and then thought he could swoop in and save me like some kind of a hero? I was not the type of girl who needed to be saved.

Movement from the creature drew my eyes from Aidan. Hissing at us as it moved, it struggled to its feet. Since I lost my flashlight in the struggle, I had to rely on the dim street lighting to study it. It resembled a hobgoblin, but bigger—much bigger. Around my height, reddish brown lizard-like skin covered the creature from head to toe, and it was probably double my weight. Long arms hung nearly to its knees, with exaggerated fingers extending from them. Its head looked small on its large, swollen body, and its face was made mostly of a sharp-tooth-filled mouth.

A freaking goblin.

I counted us lucky we hadn't had any small children

disappear in the neighborhood. Goblins were rare, much more so than their hobgoblin cousins, and had to be eliminated if they wandered into human areas. The food was too easy, and too plentiful. They were never satisfied to live in the wild after they tasted the easy life of living near humans.

The goblin got to its feet. It crouched—feet and hands on the ground—then flew at Aidan.

"Errr!" Aidan growled, as the goblin attached its mouth to his arm. He tried to shake the monster loose and hit it repeatedly with his free hand, but it held on. Goblins were the pitbulls of the otherworld.

I grabbed a rock from the dirt. Probably a decoration, it had the benefit of being softball sized. Reaching out, I yelled at Aidan, "Hold still!"

Aidan stopped moving and I took the rock and with all my strength, slammed it down on the goblin's head. I hit him two or three times, but the little bastard held on. Finally, after the fourth hit, when it felt like my fingers were going to fall off, the goblin let go.

"Cover your ears!"

Screaming for me comes in two forms. One, when I'm excited or scared or screaming in good fun. If I'm not careful—and I've learned to be very careful through the years—I can hurt people with those screams. But the other kind of scream involves real intent, a concentrated effort on my part to belt out at a level that is almost beyond what can be picked up by human ears.

Aidan took a half second to react, just enough time for me to take a deep breath. The monster picked itself off the ground, sharp teeth flashing in the moonlight, and headed back for us.

I screamed.

• • •

By the time the paramedics said it was okay for me to leave, the goblin's gooey blood had crusted on my clothes, my hands, and my hair. I gave a quick summary to the lieutenant over the phone, and told him I'd file my official report after a shower and a good night's sleep. He objected—but not strenuously—so I considered that close enough to agreement.

"Can I drive you home?" Aidan asked, as I walked away from the goblin house. He'd disappeared before backup arrived, saying he didn't want to steal my thunder. I suspected it was more because he didn't want to fill out the associated paperwork, but I respected his wish. He'd helped me, after all. I could still change my mind when I filed my official report. Probably.

"I can drive myself, thank you very much," I said.

"Well I just thought you might not want your car to smell like goblin innards for the next few months."

I looked down at my clothes and frowned. Getting goblin stench out of my car would be a challenge. I wished I'd remembered their tendency to explode when exposed to banshee screams, but it wasn't like I ran into goblins every day.

Aidan shook his keys at me. "It's a rental." He grinned.

"Fine. Thanks." Freaking goblins. I'd never run into one before, they were technically endangered. Hell, if a species as rare as a goblin could show up in a residential neighborhood so close to Chicago, wasn't it possible for something like an incubus to still be around? Granted, goblins weren't exactly extinct, but they were very rare. If someone had asked me a week before what the chances were of a goblin showing up where this one had, I would have said the chances were nil.

Trudging to Aidan's Jeep, I struggled to find a point of conversation that didn't make me sound like a pathetic little girl who'd been sad to wake up to find the guy she'd just had fan-freaking-tastic sex with gone, without a word. Nothing came to mind, so I settled for saying nothing at all.

"Look," he began. "About this morning—"

"Don't worry about it. I don't need an explanation. I'm a big girl. I didn't expect to wake up to roses and a wedding ring." *A note would have been nice though, jerk.* "How did you even find me? What, are you following me again?"

Aidan started to speak, glanced at my face, and closed his mouth. Guess I didn't look particularly open to conversation. "I heard the call come in over the radio," he said, finally.

I glanced at the portable he had propped between the seats of the car. Just my luck he'd be the first on the scene. A couple of patrol cars responded not long after Aidan, but by then the goblin had been spread over every surface of the scene.

"So this morning—"

"I said don't worry about it," I muttered through gritted teeth.

He took a deep breath and turned his attention to the dark scenery flying by his window. Fine with me.

When we pulled into my driveway I muttered, "Thanks." I opened the car door, intent on getting out of the uncomfortable situation as quickly as I could.

"Kiera," he said. "Can I use your shower?"

"The OWEA too cheap to get their agents hotel rooms now?"

"I checked out this morning. My boss is convinced the incubus has moved on. He's done it before. It's too dangerous for him here now."

"Fine." That bastard better not have moved on. I wasn't done with him yet, not even close. "But I don't have any clothes that'll fit you. You're not putting goblin blood–covered stuff in my washing machine."

He grimaced. "My suitcase is in the back. I'm thinking I'll burn these."

"Probably a good idea."

I only had one full bathroom in my house, and guest or no, I got the first shower. Besides, he wasn't exactly an invited guest, more of an unwanted refugee. While I got dressed, Aidan used the shower. I took both of our sets of clothes and sealed them in plastic bags, and then put those in a garbage bag before tossing them in my trash bin. Goblin blood could be corrosive given enough time to work at the material, and I didn't want it damaging my garbage bin. Not to mention the smell. I didn't have a place readily available to burn the material, so the trash people would have to deal with it.

"How are your ears?" I asked from my favorite spot on the couch, when he appeared from the shower, freshly dressed and once again drop-dead gorgeous.

"Still ringing a bit, but not bad."

I didn't want to talk about the fact that I was a banshee. I was too damn tired. It would bother him or not, his choice. Besides, he knew about my…heritage before he slept with me.

"About this morning—"

"I said don't worry about it." I couldn't keep the pissy tone from my voice.

"Let me finish," he said, clenching his fists to his sides. "It's been…a really long time since I've done anything close to a relationship. I usually keep things…simple."

"What does that even mean? Simple as in no sex life or simple as in sex with random strangers you never have to see again?"

The expression on his face told me all I needed to know. I turned away from him, crossing my arms. I was such a freaking idiot. He touched my shoulder and I stood up and stepped away. I didn't want him touching me. It screwed up my ability to think rationally.

"It's not simple with you, Kiera," he whispered.

"Well, sorry I screwed up your normal plan. Don't worry. I get it. I wouldn't want to complicate your life." I heard my voice catch. Mortified, I felt tears burn behind my eyes and a lump build in my throat. What the hell was wrong with me?

He moved behind me. Then he wrapped his arms tightly around me, pressing my back to his chest. His face was next to my ear. He took a deep breath, smelling my hair. It took every ounce of will I possessed not to relax and lean into him.

"I'm not a free man at the moment, Kiera, not until I catch this bastard. It keeps me from making promises—promises I want to keep." His voice was low, just above a whisper.

Then, his warmth moved from my back. The sound of cabinets opening and shutting came from the kitchen. I hugged myself, not sure how to feel.

He peeked around the doorway, coffee tin in hand. "I think we should hit up that bar, Sylvester's, tonight. If he's still in town, he might be hunting there."

"That doesn't make sense. Why wouldn't he move on to a new place? He's been seen there."

"This killer likes to hunt in familiar territory. If he's still in town, I think he'll be there. If not tonight, soon." He disappeared back into the kitchen.

"I don't remember you mentioning that tidbit when we covered what little info you have on this guy."

Aidan reappeared from the kitchen and shrugged. "Thought I did."

"And I thought you were headed out of town."

"Think I'll stick around for a day or two. I'm not convinced this guy has moved on."

"You're not staying here," I snapped.

"I didn't plan on it." Irritation laced his tone. "But we can at least check out the bar together."

I sighed and pushed myself up from the couch. Who needed sleep?

Chapter Nine

Sylvester's at night confirmed my opinion that the dive was a bar masquerading as a club. While the dance floor overflowed with half-dressed college-aged kids, the majority of their customers was older, and nursed their drinks at the bar. A few people stuck to the pool tables, and guarded them from interlopers seeking to interrupt their stream of games. The music was loud, but not so loud the folks at the tables couldn't have conversations. The place had a skeezy vibe, one that would have remained even without the 1970s decor.

Aidan followed me to one of the tables, taking the chair next to mine, and set his facing the entrance. I sat so I could keep an eye on the door, which was no doubt the same reason he chose the far side of the table as well. Not because he actually wanted to sit next to me. I pushed down a wave of irritation.

The car ride over had been uncomfortable, but at least the music covered up our lack of conversation. I spotted

Kimmy and waved. She frowned, grabbed a couple of drinks off the bar, and disappeared, heading toward the tables on the other side of the dance floor.

A waitress stopped by our table and took our order. Her gaze lingered on Aidan, annoying me enough to give her a dirty look. When I glanced back at Aidan, he grinned at me.

"So the blonde is the owner's daughter?" he asked.

"She's the one who saw Amanda and Claire Simons here with the incubus."

He did a quick check over his shoulder. "Doesn't seem like she wants to talk to you."

As our waitress approached with our beers, I touched her arm and motioned for her to come closer. When she leaned in, I said, "Tell Kimmy if she doesn't get her ass over here, I'm coming to get her."

The girl's eyes widened and she nodded. She pulled away from me and trucked back to where Kimmy stood, apparently forgetting to deliver the other drinks on her platter. As soon as she got to the bar, she grabbed Kimmy and said something in her ear, pointing at me. Kimmy looked over and I waved, giving her what Amanda used to call my scary grin.

Kimmy frowned and stomped over to our table. When she saw Aidan, she took a quick step back, her eyes wide. Then, shaking her head, she turned her attention to me, shooting the occasional glance at Aidan.

"What?" she said, not even attempting civility.

"Wow, aren't we in a mood today," I said, looking from her to Aidan. She'd recovered nicely, but his body was still tense, and he stared at her as if expecting her to pull a gun. "You guys know each other?" I asked

"Of course not," Kimmy blurted out just as Aidan muttered, "Never seen her before in my life."

I frowned at Aidan after he finally dragged his gaze from Kimmy to meet my hard stare. I raised an eyebrow at him. He crossed his arms and leaned back in his chair, as if daring me to call him a liar.

"I'm working. You're bothering me. What do you want?"

I frowned. Her attitude hadn't been fantastic before, but she hadn't seemed hostile. "I'm here about a man." I kept my blank cop face on.

"Looks like you got one."

I just stared, cop face holding steady. "Have you seen him?"

"No," she said, flatly. "I told you I'd call you if he came in." Her eyes darted to Aidan, and then she turned on her heel and walked back to the bar.

"She was lying," Aidan said.

"Thank you, Captain Obvious." *But were you lying?* "What was that about?"

"What was *what* about?"

"The way you were looking at her?"

"Suspiciously?" he asked.

I frowned at him, not entirely sure I believed him. I turned my attention to my beer. Then I scanned the crowd, looking for a man with long, dark hair.

As I sat with Aidan, I got antsier. Any second I might burst out and ask him exactly what he meant by "promises" and why he couldn't make them—whatever they might be— just because he was on the job. I needed to focus. Out there somewhere, maybe in this bar, was the man who killed my partner.

Amanda's face flashed in my mind, her long hair, the muscles she was so proud of. I missed her twisted sense of humor, and her unspoken but clear support of me and the choices I made in my life. God, I was an idiot. My partner, the closest person I'd had to a friend in years, was dead. And here I was, wondering if the guy I'd used to drown my sorrow had feelings for me. I was such a piece of work.

I got up from the table and muttered, "Keep an eye on Kimmy," to Aidan. I walked toward the crowd at the other end of the bar. The dance floor and tables on the far side of it were bathed in shadows, making it difficult to make out a lot of detail on the patrons. No one resembled the man Kimmy described. Then again, given her actions, she might have lied about that, too. I walked back across the bar, pausing to elbow one guy who got a little too close. When I reached Aidan, my mood had gone beyond the irritable funk I'd arrived in. I was well into pissed territory.

"Let's go," I said.

"You sure?"

"Yeah, he's not here."

"He might be. Later."

Kimmy stood at the bar, and she watched us as she poured a beer from the tap.

"I don't think so."

. . .

As we drove, my emotions were jumbled. The irritation remained, but my awareness of Aidan grew. I watched him in my peripheral vision. The fine muscles of his arm working as he steered, the way his jaw tensed like he was thinking about something that made him angry. His strong hands and their firm grip on the wheel. My instincts told me to trust him, even as my mind said I was an idiot for considering it.

We drove in silence, and when we got to my house I unlocked the door and left it open behind me. I struggled to find the right words. The door clicked shut, locking. I turned, meeting his dark blue eyes. Desire rushed through me. His gaze drowned me. Suppressing a gasp, I stepped away from him and looked down, fisting my hands tightly at my sides to keep myself from reaching out and touching him.

Realization hit me.

"You lied to me," I said. It wasn't a question. I'd been trying to figure out what kind of otherworlder he was and the whole time it had been right in front of my face.

"Oh?" He didn't sound surprised.

"You're an incubus." I knew it was true, but hoped somehow that I was wrong. That he'd deny it. But the pieces fit. I was like a teenager every time we were in the same room together, instantly hot and horny. That wasn't normal, no matter how attractive he was, no matter how long it had been since I'd had sex.

"I never lied about that."

My heart sank and I swallowed the lump in my throat. "Yes. You did." Here I'd been trying to work out what he was when he'd practically admitted it to me when I asked. *A sex god*, he'd said. I was so stupid.

"Why? Because I didn't tell you I'm not human? You didn't actually tell me you weren't human either, sweetheart. If I hadn't figured it out on my own, you wouldn't have told me." His voice was harsh and low, but there was no anger in it. Shivers ran down my spine at the sound; something about the timbre elicited even more of a reaction than his normal voice. Suddenly I realized that more than a tingling sensation went up and down my back, a soft touch moved there as well. I stifled a gasp at his caress. It wasn't right, but my reaction felt out of control. The realization that I was swiftly losing it finally hit me, and I stepped away from him, out of his reach unless he chose to follow me.

He didn't.

"Maybe I didn't tell you that I'm a banshee, but you knew anyway." Stay with the subject. Don't talk about the touching. Don't mention how he makes you feel.

"Not at first," he admitted. "But I figured it out pretty quickly."

"How did you know, anyway?" I turned to face him, realizing my mistake when his eyes caught me again. A chunk of his dark hair had escaped from its proper place and sat over his eyebrow. I reached out toward him to push the hair back, but caught myself before I touched him and made a firm fist at my side.

What the hell was wrong with me?

"I've…been around a while. There's a resonance in your voice. Nothing obvious, a human would never notice, but I've met banshees before. I know what to…listen for." He moved closer to me, taking my hand in his. He rubbed his thumb across my palm softly. I let him.

"Why would the OWEA send you to hunt your own kind? Isn't that a conflict of interest?" I couldn't concentrate; the light touch of his thumb distracted me, more so than such a simple touch should be. I willed myself to pull away, but try as I might, I couldn't.

"About that…" He grimaced and looked down.

I stepped back again, away from Aidan. "What? I knew there were things you still weren't telling me." He wasn't the killer; I knew that. He didn't fit Kimmy's description, but that didn't mean he wasn't a heartbreaker and a liar.

"It's just…incubi can be difficult to track and take down. I'm uniquely qualified for the job." He reached out for me again. "Just because we share the same race doesn't mean we're at all alike, Kiera. I'd no more support a rogue incubus than you'd support a rogue banshee."

"No, you just run around the country after a bad guy— leaving God knows how many thralled women in your wake. Do you get a kick out of making them fall for you with your power and then leaving them behind?"

He flinched as if I'd hit him. "First of all, my power doesn't work that way. I can elicit lust, passion, desire. A certain amount of that is part of my natural state, and I could no more block it than a lycanthrope could block the bit of wildness that lingers around them, or the fear that vampires naturally cause. If I were juiced up, I could thrall women—if I wanted to. But I can't make anyone fall in love with me. Truly loving someone, caring about them, that can't be manufactured by my powers or anyone else's." He leaned toward me and I met his gaze. "And if you really think I'm the kind of man who would use my powers like that—"

"I'm sorry." I swallowed hard. "That wasn't a fair assumption. I just—" I stopped. Telling him I was scared shitless of how he made me feel was a bad idea, for so many reasons.

I let him pull my hands into his, and as he stepped closer to me my mind and instincts continued to battle. I wasn't at all certain I could trust him, but what he said made sense. I knew I'd hunt down any otherworlder—banshee or incubus or whatever freak it might be—if I had to. I would hunt and execute them if the situation called for it. That was my job. His job, too. And he never claimed to be human, or denied his incubus heritage—he just didn't offer up the information. A private person too, I understood, even if I didn't like it.

Aidan leaned down, putting his face in my hair, his mouth next to my ear. He took a deep breath, and then sighed.

My breath quickened, and I held myself carefully still. "But you've been affecting me, haven't you? With your thrall?"

He didn't step away, but he pulled his head back so he could meet my eyes. "There is an aura that we carry as a species, just like succubi. Just like vamps and the aura of fear they carry. It isn't something I consciously control. It's just part of who I am. I can't help that. You understand that, don't you?"

I could. And I did. How many times had I wished I'd been born a normal human? Banshees were outcasts because of their nature. And though my underpowered status allowed me to live a fairly normal life, I'd never be anything but what I was. A freak trying to do the best she could with the life she'd been given.

Could I blame him for doing the same?

Something of my assent must have shown in my expression, because he moved his face back to my ear. "God, you smell good," he whispered. Touching his lips to my neck, just above my collarbone, he left small kisses in his wake as he moved his mouth up to mine.

He smelled pretty damn good, too.

Tender kisses made me squirm in his arms, and he moved

his mouth from mine and chuckled softly in my ear. Stepping back, he took my hand in his and tugged me toward my bedroom. I followed him, shooting a longing glance toward the living room floor over my shoulder.

Aidan stopped, a smile on his lips. "Don't worry, it'll be even better starting off on an actual bed."

I barely suppressed a nervous laugh. Better? How could it be better? I wasn't entirely certain I would survive *better*. But I let him pull me along when he started back down the hall.

I'd made my bed—not something I could usually claim on a weekday, so I was glad I'd taken the time. Though I was pretty sure Aidan wouldn't have minded messy sheets.

He brushed his lips over mine when he pulled me back into his arms. Soft on my back, his fingers ran lightly over my still-covered skin. I stepped back when he broke the kiss and slowly unbuttoned my blouse, conscious of his eyes on me, and of the light still on overhead. I reached the last button and then let the shirt drop to the floor, watching him expectantly.

He smiled at me, and the look was somehow warmer than his normal grin. He pulled his shirt over his head. Then pulled down his jeans, leaving only boxer briefs to cover what I didn't need my imagination to envision. His body was hard, chiseled, but not so developed he looked like the only place he spent time was the gym.

Drinking him in with my eyes, I wondered what he thought of when he looked at me. Did he see a banshee, or a woman? A niggling doubt touched my thoughts. Was I just another lay he'd barely remember a year from now?

I pushed the thought away. For better or worse, I'd

decided to sleep with him. Only time would show what he decided to do with that trust. I unbuttoned my pants, tugged them down over my hips, and let them fall to the floor before stepping out of them. Only a second passed before he stopped taking me in with his eyes. Then he took me into his arms.

He kissed me for a few moments before lifting me up against his hard chest and placing me carefully on the bed. Covering my body with his, he trailed his way down my neck, kissing and nibbling. His face was rough against my skin and I could feel he hadn't shaved in a day, at least. He slid a hand up and lightly touched my inner thighs, almost tickling, and then he palmed me. I gripped his broad shoulders, digging my fingers into his skin.

His touch was firm, but not rough, and I strained against him, trying to make him press harder. I couldn't help myself from seeking the release I knew he could grant me. But he pulled back as I pushed forward, and then moved closer again when I relaxed, torturing me.

"Kiera," he whispered, and as he pressed his hand more firmly against me, I gasped.

The rest of our clothing disappeared under his expert hands. He lowered his head to trail kisses down my side, before nipping at my hip bone.

Screw this. No way was he always going to be in control.

I pushed at his shoulders and he looked up at me, brows furrowed in confusion. But when I nudged him down onto his back and bent my head to kiss and nibble my way down his chest, tasting his slightly damp skin, his breath caught and his eyes widened. He dropped his head back when I lowered my face and licked his hip bone, biting and kissing my way to his erection. And when I took him into my mouth, he groaned.

"Yes," he said, breathless.

I tortured him with my mouth, the way he'd tortured me with his. Speeding up until he was at the brink, and then slowing down. He gripped my hair in one hand, keeping it out of my face rather than using it to direct me. He knew I needed this, needed the control, needed him to want me as badly as I wanted him.

His eyes met mine, and with a final, long lick, I released him. Settling on top, I rubbed myself against his hardness, but didn't take him inside of me.

"Kiera." He spoke my name softly, and there was the hint of a question in his voice.

I just looked at him.

"Will you let me drink from you, just a little bit?"

I tried to grasp what Marisol had said about joining with a succubus, because I knew the same rules would apply to an incubus, but my mind shied from it. He wasn't going to drain me to death, after all. But in the back of my head I wondered if the process would bond us. I buried the thought, smothering that dangerous desire.

And part of me, a small part, wanted to feel what the victims felt before they died. What Amanda felt. I would get part of him too, that's what Marisol said. If he was hiding something from me, would this reveal that? I wouldn't be helpless, after all. I wasn't under thrall. If he started to take too much, I'd show him exactly how loudly I could scream.

Just a taste, he said, and I so badly wanted him to taste me.

"Yes. Do it," I said.

If I hadn't been expecting it, I might not have noticed anything. As I edged my hips up from him, something touched me, very softly. As he eased his cock into me, something of him eased into me psychically as well. Heat built in my chest and in my stomach, and for a brief moment, I felt safe and warm and home.

Aidan distracted me from the subtle, but powerful feeling by starting an equally powerful sensation within me. I moved against him, a slow rhythm designed to torture us both, savoring the sensation of him rocking against me. He cupped my breasts as I moved, rubbing and squeezing them gently.

Finally, the slow rhythm grew to be too much. Aidan growled and flipped me over, placing himself firmly on top. I gasped in surprise and could only cling to him as he claimed control. The soft touch I'd felt when he connected to me increased in intensity, and it burned in my chest. Then spread.

Aidan pulled one of my legs up over his shoulder and buried his face in my hair. The faster he moved in me, the more the heat in my chest spread, over my breasts and to my hands and feet, and between my legs. After a few moments the heat turned to ice, but the sensation wasn't uncomfortable, just intense. I gripped his backside, digging my nails into him, while my knee pushed into my shoulder. I couldn't catch my breath enough to speak, enough to cry out. There was just him, moving so fast within me I almost couldn't hold on, and the freezing heat that threatened to burn me up.

With a burst of energy, a cry escaped my lungs. As my world exploded Aidan thrust into me once, again. He cried out, face pulling back from my hair as he tensed.

With one last shudder, he collapsed against me.

• • •

I woke up in a much better mood than the previous day, if more than a little exhausted. A side effect of letting Aidan drain me more so than a sleepless night, I suspected. But I shied away from thinking about what that might mean, and I didn't feel any different from the small bit we'd shared. After several hours of enjoying each other's company, Aidan took me to pick up my car. He was gone again by the time I got up, but he'd kissed me before he left and whispered a quick good-bye. My happy glow didn't even disappear when I realized I needed to go to the office to fill out a mountain of paperwork about the goblin kill. The number of forms literally doubled when you had to perform a field execution instead of a capture.

Piping-hot coffee waited in the kitchen, so I poured some into a to-go mug and headed for the office. I was still irritated Aidan hadn't seen fit to confide in me about his heritage, but the fact he made me coffee before he left got him a lot closer to being forgiven. Another night spent together didn't hurt his case either. And not being extinct wasn't a crime. I cursed at myself for thinking about him more than I should, but I couldn't help the warmth in my heart.

I walked into the precinct and the receptionist at the front desk gave me a puzzled look as I waved hello to her. She waved back tentatively. Wondering what her problem was, I made my way to my desk.

"You get laid or something?" a gruff voice said from behind me.

Feeling heat flood my cheeks, I didn't turn around. "What

the hell are you talking about, Aggie?"

"Well, that's the only explanation I can think of for the shit-eating grin the receptionist said you were wearing today." I could hear the smile in his voice. Nothing made Agrusa as happy as giving a fellow officer a hard time.

"Didn't you hear? Bagged myself a goblin last night. Adds a little extra skip to a girl's step." Not to mention hours of amazing sex with an incubus. I sat down, keeping my back to Agrusa. My face was probably red and it would only feed his suspicion.

"Hrmph," he said. I almost sighed in relief when I heard his footsteps retreating.

I didn't have to wipe the giant grin off my face — Agrusa's observation had done that for me. No wonder the uniform at the reception desk looked at me like she'd never seen me before. Grinning idiot. Might as well walk in humming. Nothing would drown my happy mood like paperwork. With that cheerful thought in mind, I grabbed a pen from my desk drawer and started a written description of the goblin incident. My notes got to the point where I entered the dwelling when the sound of stomping feet behind me pulled me from my work.

"You need something, Lieutenant?" I asked without turning around.

"My office, Mac."

I followed him into his office, and shut the door behind me. "Working on the goblin report. Would have done it last night but you'd have had to scrub the station for weeks to get rid of the smell."

Lieutenant Vasquez grimaced. "That's not why I need to talk to you." He gestured toward the chair in front of his desk. Taking the hint, I sat.

"Okay, then what is this about?" I kept my voice flat, even, and hoped he didn't know the full extent of my side investigation. Looking into Amanda's murder even though I wasn't supposed to would be understood, even respected. Keeping important things like the suspect's description and last known location to myself was impeding an investigation. At the very least he'd be able to take my badge. I'd be lucky if he didn't push for jail time considering how much he liked me.

"Your OWEA friend, Aidan Byrne."

"What about him?"

"There's no one with the OWEA named Aidan Byrne."

My mouth dropped and I leaned forward, gripping Vasquez's desk, ready to argue with him. I took a deep breath and hoped like hell I looked pissed, not hurt.

"Furthermore," he continued, "the OWEA has not been looking into these murders, and wasn't even aware of a connection between our victims and any others. Were you ever able to get files from this contact?"

"No," I said, my voice rough. And I hadn't asked again because I'd been more distracted by him than what he was supposed to be getting me. Dammit.

"Did you get any names?" He leaned back in his chair and studied my face.

Get a grip, Mac. "No. I didn't follow up with him, since I'm no longer on the investigation. I figured the guy would contact you." I met his eyes, keeping a firm frown plastered on, and concentrated on thinking angry thoughts. *Pissed. I'm just pissed. Nothing to see here, Vasquez. I'm not lying to you to cover my ass, not obstructing an ongoing investigation.*

Lieutenant Vasquez frowned at me. "Well, if you hear anything else from him I need to know. And get me a description ASAP. Write it up. If he's not with law enforcement, he's a suspect. Could be he's some private investigator one of the vic's families hired, but if that's the case he should be sharing information with us." Vasquez motioned toward the door and picked up his phone, dismissing me.

When I got back to my desk, it took every bit of willpower I could muster to sit down as if nothing had happened. Vasquez couldn't know I had any interest in Aidan outside of the professional. My job would be at stake. Moreover, it would be embarrassing as hell. I forced myself to finish writing my report, and then started in on the additional paperwork related to the goblin execution, fighting tears and rage every step of the way. I called Aggie in between endless forms hoping he'd have more info on Amanda's case, but he didn't pick up, so I left him a curt voice mail.

I tried to concentrate on my reports, but my flittering thoughts made focusing difficult. Why did he lie to me? If the OWEA didn't send him, then who? Could he be involved with the killer? Could he *be* the killer? Kimmy's reaction flashed in my mind. She was startled when she saw Aidan. Because she'd seen him before?

By the time I finished my paperwork and was ready to head out, it was late afternoon. I still hadn't heard from Aidan, and I hadn't bothered to call him either. I needed to sort through this before I saw him again.

If I saw him again.

My heart twinged, making me even more irate. Damned liar made me care about him. I had to work this out on my own, and find the killer. Then I'd deal with Aidan.

Provided, of course, he wasn't the killer.

"Detective McLoughlin?" an unfamiliar voice asked from behind me.

I started, almost dripping water from the paper cup I'd just filled from the cooler. But my back was to the man, whoever he was, so he probably hadn't noticed. Squaring my shoulders, I turned to face him.

He was tall, over six feet, which made him a lot taller than me. He wore a fed suit and had a fed hairstyle—neatly trimmed and combed backward with some sort of product gunked on to keep it in place. His hair was brown, as were his eyes, and he was handsome in an obvious sort of way.

I kept my cop face firmly pasted on and put my free hand on my hip. Very deliberately, I took a sip of my water.

"Kiera McLoughlin?" His eyes narrowed and he clenched his jaw, clearly annoyed.

"I'm Mac. Who are you?" It was rude, but I'd had my fill of the OWEA today, and this guy reeked of belonging to them. The fact that Aidan wasn't really with the agency notwithstanding.

He frowned at me. "I'm Bradley Greaves." He pulled his badge out of his inside jacket pocket and held the leather case open so I could see his identification. It looked just like the one Aidan flashed me the night I met him. "I'm an agent with the OWEA. I need to talk to you about the man you say has been impersonating an agent."

"I've already told my lieutenant what I know." I turned to walk back to my desk and hoped that Agent Greaves was as human as he appeared. Some otherworlders—vampires and lycanthropes especially—had very good hearing. And anyone with hearing like that would know my heart was beating so fast it was amazing the organ hadn't thumped its way out of my chest.

"Detective," Greaves said, raising his voice slightly in warning. "We're going to have this discussion, and we're doing it now."

I spun back around to face him. "Last I checked you don't have any authority over me, Agent Greaves."

"He doesn't, but I do." I mentally cringed at the voice behind me, but kept my face carefully neutral. That voice I knew. Unfortunately.

"Really? Internal Affairs feels the need to poke their nose in this?" I asked without turning around.

"We've been asked to," he said icily.

"Thank you for coming, Mason," Greaves said, voice dripping with satisfaction. "I've taken the liberty of securing us an interview room so we can speak freely."

Chapter Ten

Mason Sanderson sat at the end of the rectangular table while
Agent Greaves took his place opposite me. Mason didn't look
happy, though I couldn't think of a time when I'd seen him
with a cheerful expression. A freak squad veteran, he'd moved
to the Internal Affairs division when Lieutenant Vasquez
took over the squad. His chiseled face and dark eyes would
have been handsome on another man, quite handsome. But I
could never get around the hard edges of his expression and
the seriousness of his demeanor. I needed humor in a man.
Like Aidan with his sardonic smile and light, teasing attitude.

Fuck.

Greaves pulled me from my thoughts with a question,
but I'd missed it so I just stared at him. He stared back, pen
in hand, hovering over a legal pad.

"Just walk us through how you met the man impersonating an agent and all of your contact with him," Mason said.

"Sure. I met him when I left Rebecca Anderson's house."

"The second possible victim you know of in your jurisdiction?" Greaves asked.

"Yes. He was at my house, in my dining room, when I got home."

"This was Sunday night?"

"Yes." I couldn't keep the touch of impatience out of my tone.

"And you didn't find it odd that a law enforcement officer would break into your home?" Greaves raised an eyebrow at me.

"Of course it was odd, but he had proper identification and he seemed to have knowledge of the case." What else had he lied to me about? What else was he hiding? I needed time to think, to get my mind around what was going on.

Greaves snorted. "So you assumed that a man, who had already broken into your home, who had full knowledge about at least two murders, was on the up and up just because he had a convincing badge? What kind of cop are you?"

"Hey—" I leaned forward until I hit the table with my chest. Shit, could Aidan be the killer? No—why wouldn't he have killed me by now? Plus, he hadn't thralled me. Had he?

No.

I would have picked up on that. I would know if I were being manipulated.

"Watch your tone, Greaves," Mason cut in, raising a hand in warning.

"Come on, Mason. This guy's probably a serial killer and she's been playing nice with him, feeding him information about a police investigation." Greaves grabbed the table as if he wanted to pull it from the ground and throw it at the wall in frustration. Then he took a deep breath and released his grip, once again the composed OWEA agent.

"You have no idea what you're talking about." I kept my voice even, just barely. "I'm not part of the investigation anymore. What could I possibly have to share?" I considered, for a brief moment, coming clean about the full extent of my relationship with Aidan. It was probably my best bet for having a career once all of this came to light, and almost certainly the right thing for me to do. As a cop. But I wasn't just a cop, and dammit, if Aidan was a bad guy in all this, I was going to be the one to bring him down.

"What did he look like?" Greaves leaned back in his chair, bringing his notepad and pen with him.

I shrugged. "Dark hair, dark blue eyes."

"Handsome?"

"I guess…what the hell does that have to do with anything?" My heart sped up and I could feel sweat building on the back of my neck and between my breasts. They didn't know about Aidan and me. They couldn't. If they had I'd already be in a lot more trouble than an interview, and there was no way Vasquez would have let me out of his office without more than a small talking-to if he knew. I kept my face blank, but my heart didn't listen.

"You screwing this guy, Detective? Is that why you didn't check up on him? Didn't care to know what your honey was really up to?" The sneer on Greaves face made me want to scream until his eardrums exploded, but I didn't react. Any reaction and he'd have me.

"That's enough, Greaves," Mason warned. "You'll keep your questions to the topics we discussed or you'll leave without questioning Detective McLoughlin further."

Greaves leaned across the table and pointed his finger at

my chest. "You should have known he wasn't OWEA; running his name by our office would have taken a few minutes. Don't pretend you haven't been doing your own side investigation. You've been spotted at one of the victim's houses—"

"Amanda Franklin! That was her name. She wasn't some nameless victim." I'd lost the battle to keep my emotion from my voice, but at that point I didn't care. "She was a damn good detective. And you're right. I should have realized Aidan Byrne—or whatever the hell his name really is— wasn't OWEA the second I noticed he didn't have a giant stick shoved up his ass!"

"Why you bi—" Greaves jumped from his chair and Mason stood as well.

"Sit down, Greaves," Mason ordered, and his tone, though full of warning, was low.

I had half stood when Greaves did, and I sat back down when he did, too. Mason remained standing, arms crossed.

"You were given permission to interview Detective McLoughlin, Agent Greaves. You were not granted leave to interrogate her like some sort of criminal or attack her personally. This interview is over. If you want to talk to the detective again, you can do so through me or Lieutenant Vasquez."

Greaves opened his mouth to argue and Mason slammed his hand on the desk, palm down. Greaves jumped a bit in his chair and closed his mouth.

"Get out of here, Mac," Mason said, eyes never leaving Greaves.

I was pissed, and an argument with Greaves still felt like a good idea. But Mason outranked me, and he'd spent more than a decade in the paranormal unit. A human wouldn't have put in that kind of time. I didn't know what he was, but I was willing to bet Greaves did. And if the sweat on the agent's brow and the tightness of his jaw was any indication, whatever Mason Sanderson was, he was a scary mother.

. . .

My phone started ringing the second I left the station. I glanced down at the number, and frowned. Aidan. I ignored the call, but after the third time, I started to wonder. No calls from him the entire day while I was at the office, and now three in a row. How close of tabs was he keeping on me? After a quick stop through a fast food drive-thru, I headed back to the office, ignoring yet another of Aidan's phone calls as I pulled into the police parking lot.

"Jerk," I muttered. He'd lied to me. Lied to me and slept with me and made me look incompetent in front of my co-workers. I blinked back tears and tried to focus on anything but Aidan. But focus failed me, and I found myself opening my phone to call him back.

"Hello, beautiful." Aidan's voice was smooth. Whatever tabs he kept on me apparently didn't extend into the inter-view rooms at the police station.

"Screw you, Aidan. You lying asshole." The words spilled out before I could stop them, before I could even think about pretending I didn't know he'd lied. Before I could come up with any kind of plan other than yelling at him.

Silence greeted me on the other end of the line.

"Call me again, and I'll sic the OWEA on your ass. The *real* OWEA, not liars like you with plastic badges. Don't call me again. Don't try to find me. Don't even fucking think about me." My voice cracked, and I shut the phone with a snap. Blinking back tears, I concentrated on breathing. No crying. Not over that lying ass.

After a few minutes I had myself under control again. I wasn't going to think about Aidan, but if he had anything to do with Amanda's death, I'd nail him to the wall. Aggie hadn't returned the call I'd sneaked while going through paperwork, so poking around the office after hours seemed like my only hope of getting any information on Amanda's case tonight. Either that, or head back to Sylvester's and let Kimmy give me the evil eye all night. Or I could call Aidan back and talk to him like an adult.

Screw that.

As I dug into my fries and stared at the nearly empty parking lot around me, I considered calling Marisol. As a member of the paranormal division, she would be able to access the records. Maybe. I suppressed a sigh. No, I couldn't bring her into this. My career was most likely already in the crapper, but hers didn't have to be. It wasn't fair to drag her down with me.

But Claude held sway, and I suspected he was far more powerful than he acted. Not only was he a vampire—and despite the fact he'd never admit it, Vasquez was scared shitless of vampires—but Claude didn't really need his job. Oh, he seemed to enjoy the work, but the man drove a new quarter of a million dollar car every few months and lived in a high-rise condo in the most expensive part of town. He didn't *need* it, not like I needed to find Amanda's killer. Besides, if he wasn't willing to help me, he simply wouldn't.

I opened my phone and pulled his number from my list of division members' contact information. The phone rang several times, and then went to voice mail.

"Claude, it's Mac, call me when you get this. It's important." I flipped the phone shut and tossed it onto the passenger seat. I munched on my remaining fries and tried to think my way through the maze that this case had become.

If the witch, Natalie, was right, Amanda may very well have led her killer to her doorstep by trying to track him. That meant he wasn't just an otherworlder—he was knowledgeable about magic. I frowned and took a sip of my Coke. If what Marisol said was true, succubi—and by extension incubi—kept a piece with them of the people they drained. I wasn't entirely clear how that worked, but if draining one person to the point of death, a person who deserved it no less, had almost killed her sister—hell, had driven poor Elaine to become a shut-in for years after the incident— then what must draining so many women have done to this incubus? He had to be insane, truly mad, if he carried bits of the personalities of the dozen women he'd killed.

Well, a dozen if Aidan had been telling the truth.

I muttered an expletive and tried to focus on anything other than Aidan Byrne. But thoughts of him flitted through my mind as if summoned by my determination to banish them. I'd never had a man affect me like he did, never felt such overwhelming feelings so quickly. I stilled, a sudden thought hit me, and my stomach tensed. Could Aidan be influencing me with his incubus power, using more than just his aura, but actually consciously trying to thrall me? He shouldn't be able to do that, not unless…

Not unless he'd been draining people.

No. He couldn't be, could he? My thoughts scattered and I couldn't bring them back into focus. Amanda, Aidan, my soon-to-be-shot career, and the OWEA agent and his asshole attitude all scrambled together to muddle my thoughts.

Screw this.

I started the car and threw it into reverse. I had to do something. I'd find Claude; go to his house. It had been a year since I'd been there, when Claude had held a small party to celebrate a commendation his partner received. But I could find the place again.

Swinging out onto the road, I headed east and tried to remember what street Claude lived on. I got a few blocks before I noticed in my rearview mirror the unmarked car several car lengths behind me. A couple of turns later, I was almost certain I had a tail.

Freaking Greaves.

I gunned it and swerved hard to the right, turning down a one-way street, and then made the next left. Sure enough, the car followed me. A few more turns and I made my way into some traffic.

Ten minutes and several miles of weaving through traffic and making dangerous turns later, I'd lost the agent. I grinned and made an illegal U-turn and headed for Claude's.

The sound of my cell's ring filled the air. Sighing, I grabbed the phone, expecting to see Aidan's number. It seemed far too soon for anyone else to be calling me back the way my luck was running. And the man did not give up.

I glanced down at the number. Not Aidan, unless he was using a different phone. I frowned. Dare I answer it?

I dared.

"Hello."

"Detective McLoughlin?" The high-pitched female voice on the other end of the line was panicked.

"Kimmy?" It sounded like the bar daughter's owner, but

I couldn't be certain from two words.

"He's here!" she screeched.

"On my way." I clicked the phone off, shoved the last couple of fries in my mouth and headed for Sylvester's.

• • •

The crowd at Sylvester's pressed against me as I made my way to the bar where Kimmy stood. She crossed her arms and shifted her weight from one foot to the other, glancing around the room. Her eyes found mine and she motioned me to the side of the bar.

"Where is he?"

"He asked if he could pick me up after work. I told him to come by at eleven."

"Good job." *Way to go, Kimmy. Guess you're more than a pretty face and a pissy attitude.*

I picked a shadowed corner to sit and observed the throng of people around me. I found crowd watching infinitely more exciting than television.

According to my watch, I had two hours to kill before the incubus would return to pick up Kimmy. She handed me a glass of beer on her way to deliver drinks. Imbibing alcohol on the job was something I'd normally frown on, but one wouldn't kill me. Besides, I didn't want to be noticed, and not drinking anything in a bar might seem odd. Fully rationalized, I took a sip. Not the best I'd ever tasted, but after the crappy day I was okay with mediocre beer.

By the time I finished my drink and had waved Kimmy away when she offered me a second, it was nearing ten o'clock. My people watching degenerated into staring at the bar while wondering if Aidan was the killer, my brain fuzzy from the beer.

The pieces fit. He was an incubus, I couldn't account for his whereabouts when the murders took place, he'd lied to me—multiple times. My gut told me he wasn't the slayer, but gut wasn't everything. And, like most of my body parts, the damn thing was likely influenced by my attraction for him.

I barely registered it when someone touched my shoulder, a mere brush of fingertips. Glancing back, I saw Aidan's face. It took a second to hit me that he was there, not just in my thoughts but in person.

He smiled at me. Not the light, teasing grin he normally wore in public, but a dark smile, sexy and dangerous. His blue eyes caught mine, and his grin broadened.

"What are you so happy about?" I slurred. I paused, confused. One beer, even with how tired I was, shouldn't have made me slur.

"I'm happy to see you, of course," he said, and then touched my cheek. His hand slid down my face until his fingers came to rest under my chin, and he tipped it up so I met his eyes again. He lowered his lips to mine and kissed me.

Suddenly, all I could think of was him and how much I needed him to touch me. How much I wanted to please him. I pulled him closer, deepening the kiss. He chuckled, his mouth on mine, and pressed against me even harder. Something was different; I realized in the back of my mind that his kiss was aggressive, foreign. As he tightened his arms around me the thought flew from my head and I could only think of him.

His soft hair curled under my fingers, stuck in a long ponytail. I yanked at the stretchy band, wanting to see it down around his face.

He took my hand in his and a wave of euphoria hit me. "Let's get out of here," he whispered as his hot breath touched my ear.

Clinging to his arm, I nodded and let him lead me out the door.

• • •

I handed him my keys when he asked for them as we left Sylvester's. Heart thudding in my chest, I felt almost nauseous I was so excited. I was so lucky that this Adonis wanted to be with me, and I would have sprinted to the car if it hadn't meant leaving his side. We needed to get wherever we were going so I could show him how much I wanted him, how much I *worshipped* him. He drove us to an apartment complex not far from the bar. It was a newer building, nice and neat, and equipped with an elevator.

He pressed the up button and walked in when the *ding* sounded, holding out his hand for mine. I reached out, eager to feel his skin on mine.

"*Chère*," he whispered.

I looked up into his dark eyes and my breath flew from me. He was so gorgeous and masculine, and he wanted *me*. I gave him my hand and he pulled me to him. His lips lowered to mine as the elevator doors closed behind us. He kissed me hard, punishing, but I couldn't get enough of him, his taste. He pushed me away when the doors opened. I made a small noise in protest.

"Eager," he said. "I like that."

As we left the elevator, he yanked a set of keys from his pocket. I frowned at the unicorn keychain. The oddity of it disappeared from my mind as we arrived at a door. He unlocked it and pulled me inside, flicking on a light as we entered.

"Welcome home," he said, grinning at me.

My frown deepened. "But you don't have a home here. You're from…" I struggled to think. "Somewhere else." I stared at the slight widow's peak above his arrogant brow. It was wrong somehow. But that couldn't be right; he was perfect. I shook my head and tried to grasp my fleeting thoughts.

"Very true. But for now this is my home." His voice grew deeper. "Look at me, *chère*."

I looked, meeting his gaze. I took a quick breath. I wanted him so much. My thoughts were no longer important. He was the only thing that mattered. When he crooked a finger at me, I nearly threw myself at him.

He shoved me against the wall and kissed me, pushing his hard body on mine. Trembling, I moaned and he chuckled under my lips. I pulled him closer, and wrapped my arms around his neck to feel his hair under my hands. I yanked at the holder keeping it confined, and then pulled it off, freeing his flowing mane. As I moved back from the kiss, I took a moment to appreciate the view. His hair framed his face, trailing down over his shoulders. It would be magnificent against his naked chest. I needed to get his shirt off.

As I tugged at it, a vague warning flitted in my mind. I helped him expose his chest and pushed the thought aside. *Yes*. His dark hair draped over him, making him look even more wild and masculine. I quivered under his gaze, and then the fleeting idea that had been out of my reach since I met his eyes suddenly hit the forefront of my thoughts.

"You're not Aidan," I muttered, not sure why that fact was important.

He snarled at me, eyes narrowing, and a low growl escaped from his chest.

"You're not him," I said, more certain of it now. Still, I struggled with that bit of information's importance. I looked away from him, searching my mind.

"Look at me," he commanded, voice low and angry.

"No." I tried to move away from the wall, but his arms were on both sides of me, blocking me in.

"You will look at me, bitch!"

Power rolled over me, and my head started to turn so I could gaze at him again. I pressed my eyes shut. Sweat ran down the sides of my face. I wanted to look, so much so it was almost painful not to, but I couldn't. A cry escaped me, a small sound, weak. That bothered me. I wasn't weak, dammit.

A veil lifted from my mind, and I could think again, clearly. I lashed out, catching the man—the incubus—square in the jaw with my fist. It wasn't the best punch I'd ever landed, but his head jerked back, and he stumbled a few steps.

Staring at him, I realized that I still wanted to touch him, to take the pain from his expression. Rage filled me and I shoved the tender thought away. He was the killer. He had Aidan's face, and he'd brought me here to rape and kill me. Heat still coursed through my body when I met his angry gaze. Freaking incubi.

I felt along my back, but my gun was gone. I'd given the 9mm to someone on my way out of the bar. The memory was vague, but I was certain that person was Kimmy. The apartment, I noticed, was covered in feminine design. A flowery couch, lavender paint on the walls, a vase full of flowers on a table in the hall, next to where he'd pushed me against the wall to kiss me. This was probably her home. How long had she been keeping him here? The whole time he was in town? Or just since the heat turned up on him after he killed a cop? He was using her, enthralling her, for a place to stay and a convenient bar to find victims, no doubt.

"Look at me, *chère*," he whispered, moving closer. His voice had calmed, but his wide eyes were still wild, angry. His mouth formed a smile. He was enjoying himself. I glanced down at his jeans and flinched. Enjoying himself indeed.

I smiled back at him, and his posture relaxed somewhat. I took a deep breath slowly so he wouldn't be alarmed.

Then I screamed.

Glass shattered from the kitchen, and the incubus dropped to his knees and yelled, covering his ears. He was too late. Blood ran down the sides of his face. I reached the end of my breath and sucked in air for another scream as I inched back toward the door to the apartment. Some otherworlders were able to resist the effect of my screams, and I didn't dare release my full power in an apartment complex to ensure he would be knocked out cold. That kind of power was likely to injure Kimmy's human neighbors, and knowing my luck there'd be a sick person living next door who would be pushed over the edge from illness to death by my scream. I couldn't risk it.

As I sucked in one last breath, I reached for the door-knob behind me. Blood flowed freely down the incubus's face, and he clung to his ears and crouched, flinching away from me. Satisfied he would keep for a few minutes while I got backup, I turned away to find the doorknob, keeping my breath held in case I needed to unleash another scream. Movement flashed behind me. Something slammed against the back of my head.

The world went black.

Chapter Eleven

I awoke to the sound of a car engine purring, vibrating under my ear. I tried to move and regretted the attempt, as pain shot up to my shoulder. Tied up, my arms were behind my back, secured with handcuffs—my handcuffs most likely. My feet were tied with some sort of rope, and a rough fabric filled my mouth, kept in place with a tight gag. I struggled to breathe through my nose, pushing down the panic building in my chest.

Think. There's gotta be a way out of this. Stay calm.

I tried to move my body, to look around the vehicle, but only succeeded in moving my head. Breathing through the blackness that threatened to overwhelm me again, I checked out my surroundings. I rode in my Toyota, the gray interior flashed into view from the occasional streetlight. The asshole had shoved me into my own car.

Where was he taking me? Mentally kicking myself for turning my back to the incubus, I still couldn't believe he'd recovered so quickly, fast enough to get up off the floor and hit me with something. The vase from the hallway table? He'd moved quickly enough to get us both out of the building before the police arrived. He was quick. A banshee scream tended to get noticed and reported pretty damn fast. How had he been able to shake off my scream like that? Maybe I'd just lost my touch.

Or maybe incubi were more resistant to a half-banshee's powers than I'd like.

I'd certainly resisted his seductive abilities better than I expected. Whatever Kimmy had slipped into my drink seemed to make me instantly susceptible to the incubus' powers. Once under the thrall of an incubus, it was obviously very difficult to break free, which is why the incubus had felt safe letting even Amanda go about her day after he thralled her. Perhaps the power over me was breakable because we hadn't had sex? Or had Aidan's influence somehow protected me from the other incubus?

The car slowed to a stop, interrupting my thoughts. The grinding of a garage opening sounded. The engine cut out, and I heard the cargo door open behind me. I held still, unsure of how to fight him in my current state, but unwilling to lose any potential edge. If he thought I was still knocked out, maybe he would untie me to finish his plan. I squeezed my eyes shut, and struggled to play dead, when my instincts were telling me to squirm and fight.

I lost the battle with myself when strong arms grabbed me, and I rose up in the air, only to be caught on a shoulder. As I landed my breath flew from me, and I couldn't keep the cry from escaping my throat. My gag muffled the noise, and I silently prayed the cloth dulled it enough to go unnoticed.

"Nice to see you're going to be awake for this, *chère*."

So much for the surprise attack.

He was breathing hard. I hoped it was from the exertion of carrying me and not because he was still excited. As we passed the threshold of the garage into the house, light tan ceramic tiles flashed below me. My tile, my house. How did he know where I live? He'd done his homework. He fumbled with the light switches in the kitchen and hallway, before he tossed me onto the bed in my room. His hand snaked up my leg, moving over my stomach to cup my breast, grabbing it painfully.

"I'll be back for you soon, *chère*. Don't worry. I won't make you wait too long for it. I'm far too hungry from your shenanigans."

He disappeared and I heard him talking a few moments later from the other side of the house—the kitchen maybe. I couldn't make out the words, but I suspected he was checking in with Kimmy. I wiggled my leg, trying to get my shoes off. If I could get off one shoe, I might be able to pull a foot through the rope and free my feet. Squirming was difficult with my mouth bound, and I wanted to gasp for air, but couldn't. I forced myself to slow down so I didn't have a panic attack over my inability to breathe, and I pulled at my right shoe, using the bed and my other shoe to slowly work it off.

Sudden movement caught my eye and I cried out, almost silently because of the gag. He was back, and there was nothing I could do to protect myself. Desperate, I struggled in vain against the ropes and cuffs.

"Shhhh…" he whispered in my ear. "Hold still, Kiera."

I began my struggles anew at his words. Hold still, my

ass.

He touched my legs, and I opened my eyes to see him pushing on them with his hand, his other hand working the bonds with something—a knife? Suddenly the pressure lifted, and I could move again. I pulled them back to kick him, when his clothes caught my eye. They were different. Surely he hadn't taken the time to change? There was no blood on his face, and he backed away from me slowly, hands in the air to show he meant no harm. His hair was short.

Aidan.

"Keys?" he mouthed.

I shook my head. My cuff keys had been in my gun holster, which I'd handed off to Kimmy. But I had my legs, and most importantly, my voice.

The sound of the incubus yelling, and then the slam of something—probably my phone—hitting the wall, distracted Aidan. Then he reached out and pulled me up from the bed, onto my feet. I staggered for a moment, and he held me until I gained my balance. He ran his hand along the side of my face, trying to find room to fit the blade under the gag.

Then, Aidan was gone, flung across the room. The other incubus stood over him, knife dripping blood in his hand. I'd never heard that incubi were preternaturally strong, but I'd be willing to bet they were now. At least ones who'd recently gorged on the life force of their victims.

"Aidan?" The incubus sounded confused, as if he wasn't entirely certain he recognized Aidan.

I struggled with my gag, pulling the side of my face across my shoulder, trying to dislodge it. The incubus had secured it well. The cloth cut into my skin, and it wouldn't loosen.

The incubus knelt by Aidan. "I should have known they

would send you after me. How many years have you hunted? Did they think I would hesitate if they sent you? They should have known better." He leaned in and I could barely hear him. "We don't need anyone else, Aidan. My women and me, we're together always. We don't need you, brother." The incubus continued talking to him, so softly that I couldn't make out the words. Then he held the blade up like some sort of horror film bad-guy ready to dispense the killing blow.

My chest tightened. I couldn't scream, couldn't shoot him or strike with my fists—I was powerless. Powerless to help Aidan. Powerless to avenge Amanda. Powerless to save myself.

No.

I ran at the incubus and did the only thing I could think of—swinging my foot out, I kicked him in the side with all the strength I could muster. It wasn't much with my cramped legs and cuffed arms.

One kick, two, and the incubus fell to his side just as I lost my balance and landed on my back, gasping in pain against the gag in my mouth as my trapped arms twisted painfully under my weight.

Spots flashed and I blinked several times to clear my vision. Sudden pressure hit my legs, and I looked up to see Aidan—wrestling with the incubus for the knife.

The incubus struck out with an elbow, catching Aidan in the jaw, stunning him. He got his knee between them, and then pushed hard, sending Aidan flying across the room. Definitely abnormally strong.

I kicked out, striking the incubus in the head with my heel. He turned to look at me, and only a flash of rage registered before Aidan, stumbling to his feet, used the distraction to grab the knife. Shoving his arms down, he pushed the blade into the incubus's neck.

He twitched and tried to shove Aidan off, coughing. Blood flew from his mouth and spotted Aidan's face. Aidan grimaced and pushed the knife down further, cutting into the creature's neck. The incubus mouthed a word at Aidan, and then went still.

• • •

The first set of uniforms came in and uncuffed me. Aidan followed me out to the front porch, but kept his distance. It seemed like only minutes later Claude and his partner, Astrid Holmes, arrived on scene. Astrid held back, talking to one of the uniforms, but Claude made a beeline for me.

"I got your message," Claude told me as he shot a suspicious glance at Aidan.

"He's okay," I muttered, knowing Claude would hear my soft tone.

Claude nodded. "We should get you to the hospital."

"No, I'm fine."

He frowned but didn't argue with me. "What happened?"

I told him an abbreviated version of the events of the night, still trying to wrap my brain around what I was going to tell Lieutenant Vasquez and Internal Affairs. I decided coming clean was probably best, or close to clean anyway. None of the personal stuff that had happened between Aidan and me was anyone's business but our own. I'd just have to think of how to frame it right so Vasquez didn't fire me on the spot.

Claude nodded as I finished my story. "Well, killing the incubus complicates things, but we should still be able to ID him as the murderer, since all of the standard oh-dubs were run on Amanda and the victim before her."

"Rebecca," I muttered.

"Yeah, well. So long as the energies match, you should be in the clear on this." He glanced at Aidan. "Not sure about your friend, though. Do you know who he's working for yet?"

I shook my head and Claude crossed his arms, keeping his gaze firmly planted on the incubus. A few seconds later, paramedics were treating Aidan and asking me what seemed like a million questions. They wanted to take me to the hospital, but I refused. I might as well deal with Vasquez now, or he'd just have time to think of more questions to ask me when I did finally have to face him.

Vasquez himself showed up nearly twenty minutes later, and I didn't notice him at first because I was busy watching Aidan. He'd settled into a corner of the room, carefully noting the activity around him, but reticent. He wouldn't meet my gaze, and I was about thirty seconds away from smacking him and demanding answers when Vasquez stomped up my steps.

Claude fielded him for a few seconds. I couldn't hear what he told the lieutenant, but whatever he said, it transformed Vasquez's expression from wild-eyed raging to a solid frown line that generally meant your ass, but not your badge. A bit of tension left my neck at the change, but when he pushed by Claude and stalked toward me, it returned.

"What the hell happened here, Mac?" His voice boomed over the rest of the noises surrounding us, and even Aidan glanced over. Great, now he wanted to pay attention?

"I got a call with a lead—"

"Oh just a random call, huh? From whom? How'd they know to call you?"

"I—"

"And Sylvester's huh? I guess I don't look like such a damned idiot now do I?"

I blinked. "What are you talking about?"

He shook his head. "You went into that club without even checking it out? Who do you think owns the damn place? The Chevaliers, that's who. The damn bloodsuckers you didn't even want to interview."

Shit. That connected them to at least two of the victims. Claire Simons worked with Nicolas Chevalier, and Kimmy worked at a club the family owned. Was there a connection to the other victim that we didn't know about?

"We don't have anything real that'll stick to them, nothing beyond a tenuous link. And you're not going to be the one looking for that connection either."

"Now wait—"

Vasquez threw up a hand, halting my argument. "I told you to stay off this case. You were too close to it. And what did you do? You went out, disobeyed my orders, and almost got yourself killed!"

"I had to—"

"What? You had to what? What did you have to do that was more important than your life? Than the lives of your fellow officers? Because that's what you risked with this game of yours. You put everyone at risk, including yourself!"

"What I had to do was catch her fucking killer!" I snarled. "And I did! What the hell have you done today?"

Vasquez stared at me for a second and for the last half of that moment I thought his fist would rise and he would take a swing at me. But then he threw his head back and laughed, and the sound reverberated off the walls of my porch. The noise was even louder than his yelling earlier, and I couldn't do anything but stare.

• • •

By the time the police left my house, the sun peeked over the horizon. They'd questioned Aidan and me, separately, for hours. Saving my life was likely the only thing that kept him from being questioned at the precinct. That he looked exactly like the killer didn't help him, and the fact he'd impersonated an OWEA officer was something the police couldn't take lightly. But he saved one of their own, which bought him something—the night, at least.

"You okay?" I asked Aidan, when we were finally alone. Covered in blood, he looked like he needed a shower as badly as I did.

"I'm fine," he said. "The knife wound was superficial."

So I'd been told. "Good. They caught Kimmy."

He nodded. "I heard. Good thing." His jaw muscle twitched. "It sounds like he's had her under thrall off and on for weeks, screwing with her memory, bringing her in and out of his influence. With how powerful he was, and that kind of time…I don't think she'll ever be right, Mac."

"Her memory? Is that why she willingly told me about him even though she was probably already thralled?"

"Could be he made her forget when he wasn't around her, or he might have told her to pass on that info for some reason. It's hard to know for sure given his state of mind."

I shivered. Even the idea that someone could mess with a person's memories was chilling. "At least we got him. He won't be hurting anyone else. OW measures can match him loosely to the other victims—Amanda and Rebecca, at least. Between that and my kidnapping and Kimmy's...state of mind, it should be an open and shut case."

We sat on my porch, silent for a few minutes, watching the sun inch into the morning sky. My whole body hurt, and I was exhausted, but I couldn't bring myself to break the silence. I stretched my legs out, reaching from the top step where I sat, to the bottom step. Aidan looked to be in a similar state. His face was tense, and darkness encircled his eyes. He sat with his knees under his chin, arms wrapped around his legs.

"You lied to me. So fucking much." My voice was flat. Exhaustion had siphoned off most of my rage, but a weight pressed against my chest.

"I'm sorry. I'm so sorry, Kiera. I just—" He swallowed.

"I don't know if I can trust anything that comes out of your mouth."

"I didn't want to lie to you!"

"Then tell me the truth now." My voice broke. I concentrated on breathing. I would not fucking cry.

"Quinton was my brother," he said, finally. "He wasn't... stable. He was never quite right, odd even when we were kids. We figured out something was really wrong when girls started going missing in our hometown—ones he'd been seen with. I realized later that he was getting worse because of the women he'd killed—absorbing too much can be dangerous, but it packs a hefty punch of power." He let out a heavy sigh. "By the time the locals made the connection and called us, he'd moved on."

"Who is us?" The pain in his voice drained the anger from me. I wanted to reach out and touch his shoulder, comfort him, maybe take some of the pain out of his face. But I needed answers.

"Technically, we are part of the OWEA, but we don't answer to the normals or report through the standard channels. Our records are separate from the other divisions of the OWEA. Regular agents can't access them. We're sent into situations that it would be...awkward for humans to know about."

"I get plenty of cases where otherworlders have killed normal humans. I've never seen you people before." But it made sense. No wonder Greaves couldn't find a record of Aidan in the OWEA.

"Like I said, we're called in when things need to remain discreet. Special circumstances."

"What was so special about this case?"

"Other than the fact that incubi are supposed to be extinct, you mean?"

I blinked. I'd forgotten that, but it still didn't make sense. "Yeah, other than that."

"We've built up our numbers enough to go public again, as a registered subspecies. Coming out as the result of an investigation into a serial killer isn't the best way to show ourselves. Worst-case scenario, they could categorize us as subhuman, though even with this coming out party, I doubt that'll happen. But it would have been nice not to come out by way of a serial killer."

"So much for avoiding that. You'll be lucky if this story

isn't on every channel by now, incubus."

"I know." He put his face down onto his knees. "What's done is done. We'll just have to deal with it."

"Super special cover up?"

He shrugged, cocking his head to look at me. "That's not my problem anymore. My team is strictly an investigative agency, but with fewer rules than standard OWEA divisions."

"What? Like the CIA or something?"

"Yeah, I guess that's a pretty good parallel. Not as much bureaucracy or personnel. Not as many noses in our business." He touched his nose playfully.

"Ah." *There you go, Mac, kill him with your wit.* "Why didn't you tell me any of this sooner? And don't give me any crap about being sworn to secrecy."

He shook his head. "I couldn't tell you, for reasons I can't even confide in you now. But mostly the reasons weren't official." He kept his eyes pointed anywhere but at me. "I wanted to keep you safe, and it seemed safer to keep you gathering a bit of information here and there—"

"To help you with your investigation, you mean," I snapped.

"Yes, but not to keep all the glory or anything. I just…" His jaw clenched, and he paused as if searching his mind for the right way to say what he needed to. "I'd seen what he'd done, Kiera. I couldn't let that happen to you." He glanced up, meeting my eyes for a brief moment before looking away again. "I knew you were special, the first night I met you. I couldn't stand the thought of him getting his hands on you. And after he proved he could take someone as strong as your partner—" Aidan drew a deep, ragged breath. "I wish…"

"What?" I met his gaze and he looked away.

"I wish you hadn't seen him. It must feel—I mean, do you look at me and see the monster who attacked you?"

I scooted closer to Aidan and pressed two fingers under his chin, prodding him to look me in the eye. His normal grin was gone, replaced by a frown that cut across his features. He looked tired, and sad. I didn't like it.

"Hmm…your hair is all wrong. You're missing a certain crazy glint in your eye. Sorry bub, not seeing it."

For a moment he stared at me, jaw slack and eyes wide. Slowly, a smile overtook his face and my heart warmed. He leaned forward and kissed me, a soft touch, testing.

I kissed him back, tugging him closer to make it more interesting. When he finally pulled away, we were both out of breath. The morning air felt cool against my suddenly hot cheeks.

Giving me his normal grin, he looked me up and down. "Shower?" he asked, wiggling his eyebrows.

I laughed, and tension released from my chest. "I'll meet you in there."

As Aidan pushed himself up and went into the house, I watched the sun fully reveal itself on the horizon. Amanda was gone, but her killer no longer threatened the lives of other women. She would be proud, and I could take comfort in that. Justice had been served. A very hot man waited for me in my house. And the sun was shining. I smiled and headed for the shower.

Acknowledgments

There are so many people I owe a thank you for their help and encouragement with this project. I want to give a huge thanks to:

My family, for never doubting I could do anything I set my mind to. You've all been amazingly supportive, from reading first drafts to being impressed with all of my small steps forward. A special thanks to my mom, Judy Lopez, for never laughing at my sex scenes—where I could hear her, anyway. And thanks to my cousin, JonEll, for reading an early draft of *Banshee Charmer* and encouraging me to submit it.

My husband, Sash, who accepts my crazy writing hours in stride, and has been willing to entertain himself virtually every evening and weekend for the last year and a half.

Regan Summers, my critique partner, without whom I would not have made it so far as a writer as quickly as I have. You are not only amazing when it comes to helping me improve my work, but you also inspire me with your stories. Without your encouragement, I fear this whole process would have driven me crazier than I already am. Thank you for always being willing to lend a caring ear, or a swift kick in the butt—whichever you deem required at the time.

Joshua Roots, my fantabulous beta reader, who not only improves my work, but is also amazingly supportive of my crazy ideas. Thank you, my friend, for your help and your humor.

Barbara Rogan, and my workshop group, for helping me strengthen my writing. Barbara, your insightful criticism and encouraging words have helped me more than you'll ever know. Thank you.

My editor, Kerry Vail, for your dedication and encouragement. You have helped make this story into something I am very proud of, and never made me feel dumb when answering all of my newbie questions. Thank you for caring so much about my story and characters, and laughing at my silly jokes. You have made what could have been an arduous process into something enjoyable.

The rest of the Entangled team, especially Heather Howland, for seeing potential in my story and helping me develop and market it.

About the Author

Tiffany Allee currently lives in Phoenix, AZ, by way of Chicago and Denver, and is happily married to a secret romantic. She spends her days working in Corporate America while daydreaming about sexy heroes, butt-kicking heroines, and interesting ways to kill people—for her books, of course. Her nights are reserved for writing and bothering her husband and cats (according to them). Her passions include reading, chocolate, travel, wine, and family.

Find out more at: http://www.tiffanyallee.com

Don't miss the rest of the Files of the Otherworlder Enforcement Agency *series...*

SUCCUBUS LOST

LYCAN UNLEASHED

VAMPIRE GAMES

Also by Tiffany Alee

DON'T BITE THE BRIDESMAID

DON'T BLACKMAIL THE VAMPIRE

TEMPTATION BY FIRE

www.ingramcontent.com/pod-product-compliance
Lightning Source LLC
Chambersburg PA
CBHW021013180626
46814CB00003B/1271